Matron of Paris

The Story of Saint Genevieve

Phillip Campbell

TAN Books
Gastonia, North Carolina

Cover design by David Ferris—www.davidferrisdesign.com.

Cover image by Jim Starr.

Interior illustrations by Blueberry Illustrations
www.blueberryillustrations.com.

Library of Congress Control Number: 2022939052
ISBN: 978-1-5051-2322-7
Kindle ISBN: 978-1-5051-2323-4
ePUB ISBN: 978-1-5051-2324-1

Published in the United States by
TAN Books
PO Box 269
Gastonia, NC 28053
www.TANBooks.com

Printed in the United States of America

To Jesse Griffiths,
In thanksgiving for her feedback, prayers,
and lively interest in this project

Contents

Introduction

Saint Genevieve of Paris was one of the most extraordinary saints of the Early Middle Ages. The dates of her life are contested—some place her birth around 419 and her death in 512, while others assign her a slightly shorter life from around 422 to 500. Regardless, it's certain that she lived during a time of profound transformation as the Western Roman Empire was collapsing. Born a citizen of the Roman Empire, she died a subject of the medieval Kingdom of France. Living in this part of the world at this point in history brought her into contact with powerful, infamous, and holy people, including Saint Germanus of Auxerre, Kings Childeric and Clovis, Queen Clotilde, and many more.

Authentic sources on the life of Genevieve are scarce. A hagiography was written after her death that contains the main points covered in this book: her upbringing as a shepherdess in the village of Nanterre, her influential meeting with Saint Germanus as a girl, her religious life in Paris, and the great deeds she facilitated during the transition of Paris from Roman to Frankish control. Anything else required artistic license to fill in the gaps. Thus, this book is not a biography or history in the strict sense but a tale of historical fiction loosely woven around the few certain details we know about Genevieve (that her vocation was first identified by Saint Germanus, that she relieved Paris during a siege, that she was influential with the Frankish kings, helped build a church, etc.). But much of the specifics were the creation of my own imagination, with context supplied by what we know of the early days of the Merovingian dynasty.

Since so much has been filled in, please try not to get too hung up on dates and the convergence of different historical events. So little is known about the specifics of these events that it proved impossible to line everything up with rigorous exactitude. It is best to read this as a book of inspiration, for Saint Genevieve truly lived one of the most inspirational lives of her age or any age.

Saint Genevieve, pray for us!

Chapter 1

All Is Quiet in Nanterre Tonight

The River Seine wound cross the bleak country like a gray serpent. Wind rattled the branches of the ancient oaks along the riverside, dropping the last of their colorful autumn leaves into the flowing current. Little Genevieve rubbed her fingers together and breathed on her hands. Her woolen shawl did little to keep out the cold, but she and her father, Severus, had not expected to be out this long. He struggled over the half-frozen mud along the Seine's banks, his eyes scanning the ground.

"The tracks lead this way," he grumbled, pointing to an embankment that jutted out into the river some distance ahead. He trudged forward, stumbling and falling into the mire, his legs now browned in mud from the knees down. "When I catch him, he'll be dinner!"

Genevieve could not help but snicker. Her father was prone to grumbling and bouts of anger, but at heart he was a good man. "You're not going to butcher him," she said. "We need his wool to sell to the duke."

"Depends," shrugged Severus. "If I have to stay out here much longer, Duke Victorinus's army is going to be a few tunics short this spring."

"Papa, I think I see him!" Genevieve pointed. "Look past the embankment there, on that sandbar in the river."

Severus squinted into the distance. His daughter was right. A few hundred yards up, the embankment stuck out into the Seine like a finger pointing, it seemed, to the wayward sheep.

"How did he get out there?" asked Genevieve.

"Who knows? I've been a shepherd all my life, and I cannot figure them out. Well, let's go get him."

Father and daughter pressed through the partially frosted mud toward the embankment. The wind had picked up a bit and was stinging cold. The sky was a foreboding gray blanket of cloud. Genevieve walked with her hands tucked into her armpits, her blond hair whipped by the sporadic gusts. Severus seemed unperturbed by the cold, focused only on retrieving the animal.

As they approached the bank, they could hear the creature's bleating. The sandbar was about twenty feet out into the river, but the water was only ankle deep.

"Dumb animal!" Severus scoffed. "It walked out to the sandbar and is too stupid to walk back."

"That's why sheep need a shepherd," Genevieve said calmly.

Her father nodded. "Well, now I must do a shepherd's duty. Wait here, child."

He waded out into the shallow waters. Despite the muck and the cold, Genevieve was disappointed at being left behind. Trudging out to the sandbar looked like a fine little adventure. Nonetheless, she watched from the bank, her father growing more and more frustrated with each muddy step. The earth made a deep sucking sound every time he pulled one of his legs out. The animal looked blankly at Severus, bleating at him.

"A fine mess you've caused us today!" he yelled as he stumbled onto the sandbar. Taking the animal by the collar, he dragged it into the water. The sheep resisted, hesitant to set foot into the current. "C'mon, you blasted animal!" Severus called. But the more he pulled, the more the sheep dug its feet in.

"Be gentle, father!" called Genevieve. "He's scared!"

"He's right to be!"

Severus placed both hands on the animal's collar and yanked. But the cold had stiffened his fingers, and he could not maintain a firm grip. Severus slipped and fell flat into the water. "Arghhh!"

Genevieve hiked up her tunic above her knees and stepped into the river. She was light and small; thus, she did not sink into the mud as her father had. She reached her father quickly, helping him to his feet.

"Cursed animal!" he growled.

"He's not cursed. He's just confused." She turned to the animal. "Isn't that right?" The sheep bleated in agreement. "Poor sheep. Look at his wool, Papa! He's covered in thorns and mud. He must have had quite a day."

"Poor sheep? Look at me!" He gestured to his mud-drenched body.

"And poor Papa!" Genevieve said, smiling at her father. "Shall we try again?"

Genevieve remained in the river, now taking the lead from her father. Together, they were able to coax the sheep slowly to follow them. Genevieve's tunic eventually became as muddy and wet as her father's clothes, but they finally reached the shore.

"Let's hurry," said Severus, shivering. "It's starting to get dark, but maybe we can still get back to Nanterre in time for supper."

Father, daughter, and sheep gravitated away from the river in search of firmer ground. The road home ran parallel to the Seine, a crushed gravel path connecting Nanterre with Paris and the towns beyond. Genevieve's feet were soaked and painfully cold. She tried to distract herself by looking at the scenery, the land stretched up from the Seine in a broad, sloping field dotted with shrubs, lined at the crest with cypresses.

"I don't think I've ever been this far down the road," Genevieve said, looking up to her father.

"I think not. And that is the way it should be. This road is no place for an eight-year-old girl to be."

"Why, Papa?"

"Let's just keep moving."

Genevieve knew when to not press her father too hard on something. She pulled her shawl over her head as she'd seen the old peasant women do, to calm her hair flapping in the wind and shield her from the cold.

I can't wait to sit by the fire at home and eat some hot dinner, she thought.

Several minutes later, a low rumble came up the road from behind them. Genevieve started to turn, but Severus grabbed her by the arm. "Get off the road."

"Why?"

"Just move," he ordered. With Genevieve's arm in one hand and the sheep collar in the other, Severus dragged the party off the road as the rumbling came closer. It soon became clear it was the sound of horses galloping.

"Who's coming, Papa?"

"Hush, child!"

He pulled his daughter down behind a thick patch of brambles and tucked the sheep under his arm, trying to keep it still. The sheep acquiesced, munching quietly on some brown grass.

The galloping grew louder . . . louder . . . louder.

Through the weeds, Severus and Genevieve saw a column of horsemen speeding up the road, riding two-by-two. They were helmeted, wearing long tunics covered in scale mail, and bore circular shields upon their backs. They rode with determination, heads down and red cloaks billowing behind them.

"About a dozen of them," Severus mumbled. "*Vexillationes*."

"Who?" whispered Genevieve.

"*Vexillationes*. Roman cavalry officers. Seen a lot of 'em on the road these days. At first, I thought they might have been Goths or Franks."

"So, they're not bad?"

"No, no," her father said reassuringly. "They're on our side. They're here to protect us from the barbarians."

The horsemen sped past Genevieve and Severus, oblivious to their existence behind the bushes. A moment later, they were out of sight.

"All right, let's go," said Severus. The three returned to the road and resumed their journey.

"Will they come to Nanterre?" asked Genevieve.

"I doubt it. There're more important things afoot than anything going on in a little village like Nanterre. The emperor just appointed a new *magister militum*. Troops are being shuffled around. New commands being assigned. Barbarians on the move. Everything is all mixed up."

"What's a . . . *magister*?"

"*Magister militum*. Master of soldiers. He is the head of the army. It's his job to fight the barbarians."

This talk of soldiers, battles, and barbarians filled Genevieve's head with images of wild adventure. She turned and looked behind her, down the road whence the soldiers had come. The mundane gravel path now looked perilous. She wondered what other exploits were waiting at the road's end.

As darkness enveloped the land, the world seemed to grow silent, save for the crunching of their feet on the gravel. Genevieve liked this sound; it was earthy, wholesome. But the cold was terrible, her wool tunic offering little protection against the November chill, and her feet ached, covered in nothing but some leather wraps, soaking wet and chaffing against her raw ankles.

The sheep, too, was sluggish. Severus stopped several times to goad it on before finally heaving the beast up upon his shoulders. The sight of her father carrying the sheep brought an image to the little girl's mind.

He looks like the mosaic of Christ the Good Shepherd in our church.

Her father was a hulk of a man—not too tall but broad shouldered with bulky arms and legs as thick as tree trunks. Severus's neck was a single chunk of muscle, such that his pace did not slacken one bit with the sheep upon his shoulders. To Genevieve, his power seemed infinite.

The first stars were twinkling in the deep blue firmament when they crested a hill, bringing a small village into view. "Ah, there is home," said Severus. "I can't wait to get out of these clothes and drink some warm broth."

Nanterre was a small assemblage of mortared stone houses with thatched roofs clustered upon a plain east of the Seine. Nanterre looked quaint and peaceful under the starlight, little white wisps of smoke ascending from rows of chimneys, the fires beneath them shining with an orange glow from within the homes.

Father, daughter, and sheep finally passed a large stone that marked the edge of the family's field. Genevieve and her parents lived in a cottage on the outskirts of town. As shepherds, they required more space for pasturing their flock. The family's fields were bounded by a fieldstone wall that ran along the length of the road from the boundary stone into town.

As soon as they reached the wall, Severus unceremoniously dumped the sheep over it.

"We'll clean him up tomorrow," he grumbled.

The family homestead was a squat stone structure nestled on a hillside. It was a poor place, little more than a hovel, but it was home—and Genevieve adored the view, where one could see all the homes of Nanterre huddled beside the Seine. In the summer, the colors of the fields and forests beyond were radiant, colorful wildflowers bursting up among the grasses, and the Seine sparkling blue, not gray like it was today. Behind the cottage, the hillside sloped up to the heights of Mont Valérien, the mountain that cast a shadow over the town.

Genevieve threw open the cottage door. "Mama, we're home!" she cried.

Her mother was busy stirring a pot on the hearth.

"Genny!"

Mother and daughter ran to embrace one another. Feeling Genevieve's dampness, she asked, "What on earth happened to you? Where is your father?"

"Right here," groaned Severus as he stumbled through the door.

"Mommy, we had an *adventure*!" said Genevieve, eyes beaming.

"Is that so?"

"More like we froze half to death dragging that stubborn sheep out of the Seine," Severus huffed.

Severus and Genevieve were soon clothed in fresh garments, and everyone huddled around the fireplace to warm themselves and relax. Genevieve loved her nightgown, a soft white garment of woven linen. She felt like an angel wearing it. Severus sat in a chair, soaking his feet in a basin of warm water while slurping from a steamy cup.

"Fine broth, Gerontia," he said to his wife.

"There's not much to it," she said. "Just a little salt, and I used the rest of the turnips."

"To a frozen man, this might as well be the nectar of paradise." He gulped down another mouthful.

"Here you go, dear," Gerontia handed Genevieve her own cup. Genevieve made the sign of the cross over the broth and drank it gratefully. Her mother, meanwhile, sat behind her, grooming her matted hair with a bronze comb. "I can't imagine what you two got into today," she said while she struggled with the girl's knotted locks. Genevieve didn't seem to mind; she was content sipping her broth and watching the flames cast dancing shadows about the cottage walls.

"Mama, did the Romans come here tonight?"

She shook her head. "No, I don't think so. I went to vespers earlier, and I didn't see anything. Did something happen out there?"

"Just a routine patrol," Severus said. "Some officers on the move from here to there. Nothing to fret about."

The tone of his voice seemed more concerned than he let on. Both his wife and daughter noticed but said nothing.

Suddenly, their repose was interrupted by a loud thud at the door. "Gerontia? Severus?" a voice called. "It is Mucianus."

"Ah, Deacon Mucianus!" Gerontia said with a bit of relief. She rose to open the door.

"Peace and grace to you in Christ Our Lord," the deacon said as he walked in. All rose to greet him—Severus standing in place with his feet still in the basin.

"Please, won't you sit and stay awhile, Mucianus?" said Gerontia.

"You're too kind!" said the deacon, an older man with curly wisps of white hair sitting like a crown upon a tonsured head. "But I've only come to drop off some food." He threw back his cloak to reveal a large sack.

"We're much obliged, Mucianus," said Severus.

"I know things are a little tight for plenty of us now. I've been taking up a collection, and people have been generous. Let's see, what do I have here? A few strips of salted pork, a loaf of bread. A cluster of olives . . ." He pulled each item from his sack and handed them to Gerontia and Genevieve as he spoke. ". . . and a few leeks. Not much, I know."

"It's more than enough," said Gerontia gratefully. "We are very blessed by your visit." Genevieve dutifully took the food and put it away while the adults talked.

"Things have been hard for me as well," the deacon told her parents. "Nanterre has been nine months without a priest now since Thaumastus died."

"Have you spoken to the bishop recently?" asked Gerontia.

The old deacon sighed. "Marcellus of Paris is a holy man, but he has much to deal with. The wars of the Goths and Franks. The political chaos of the empire. Rumors of the Huns massing on our eastern borders. Outbreaks of plague. Feeding the poor and caring for the orphans. Not to mention the Pelagian heretics causing trouble out west. It feels like the Church is carrying the burden of the entire world these days. I've written him, but Nanterre is just not a priority with all that's going on. Hopefully, by Christmas I'll have news."

"Mucianus," said Severus, "I saw a troop of *vexillationes* on the road this evening. Have you heard of any goings on in the region?

"The cavalry officers are out and about, are they? Thank goodness they didn't come through the village. The last thing anybody wants is Nanterre mixed up in any trouble. There's plenty going on—the emperor just made Flavius Aetius *magister militum* of the west. But that's far away from here. No, all is quiet in Nanterre tonight."

"God keep it so," prayed Severus.

"Indeed!" agreed Mucianus. "Well, I must be on my way. Shall we pray?"

The deacon made the sign of the cross, prompting the family to do the same.

"Let us beseech the Lord to prosper our days, keep us in grace, and remember our spiritual and temporal needs: *Pater noster, qui es in coelis . . .*" he began the Lord's Prayer in Latin. The family prayed along with folded hands. Genevieve had learned this prayer when she was very little and recited it every day since. While praying, she glanced at her father. The powerful man who had carried a sheep home on his shoulders only hours ago now looked docile and meek, his head bowed, his eyes closed, his blistered hands folded.

"Amen!" said Mucianus, concluding the prayer. "Good night, everyone. Sleep in the grace of Christ." With that, he disappeared into the night, making his rounds to do good elsewhere.

An hour later, Gerontia lay Genevieve down for bed on a small straw cot in the corner. It was not much, but it was cozy. Beside the bed there was a little notch hollowed out of the stone wall. There Genevieve kept a small carved statue of Christ with a candle. Her mother struck the flint and lit the candle for the girl. "The light of Christ keep thee this night," she said, pulling the woolen blanket up over Genevieve. "You had quite a day today, didn't you?"

"Yes, Mama. But it was fun!" The girl paused, her countenance dropping a little. "Although, I'm not sure if Papa had fun."

ACHOO!

Severus's sneeze boomed from across the room. "Blasted animal," he muttered to himself. Gerontia and Genevieve snickered.

"Goodnight, darling," her mother kissed her forehead.

"Goodnight, Mama."

Genevieve rolled over on her side, facing the wall. It was so good to finally stretch out under a warm blanket. Her tired eyes were fixed on the candle's gentle glow and the crudely carved image of Christ that it illumined. As her mind drifted off to sleep, she whispered, "Lord, I liked the adventure we had today. I want to have more adventures."

Chapter 2

The Visit of Germanus

In the following days, the trees became bare and the fields brown. The forested slopes of Mont Valérien turned foreboding as the naked limbs of the trees seemed like clawed hands reaching up into the bleak sky. Occasionally, snow fell from the clouds, blown over the hills and fields round Nanterre like fine dust. The Seine was black and motionless save for a few ducks gliding upon its surface.

Everyone in Nanterre was occupied making final preparations for winter. The swineherds were finishing their autumn slaughter and smoking their pork in little shacks on the outskirts of town as fishermen salted their catches by the riverside. The village's few merchants drifted back from the Paris markets, gossiping with the locals about events abroad. The farmers stored away their crops for the winter, sending portions of their harvest as taxes to Duke Victorinus and selling the surplus in town.

For Genevieve's family, this was the time to prepare the sheep for their winter pasturage. The flock needed to be moved from the fields over to the slope of Valérien. There in the mountain's tree line, Severus had constructed a series of rude lean-to shelters made of pine boughs and thatch. Here the sheep would huddle and wait out the winter, fed by the family's stores of alfalfa.

On the appointed day, Severus, Gerontia, and Genevieve bundled themselves beneath layers of tunics, donned thick wool socks, and led the flock to its winter quarters. Moving the sheep did not take so long, but the family also had to repair the enclosure to keep them from wandering, and that took considerably more time. The snow had begun to fall, and everyone's hands were purple and stiff while they worked on the stone wall that would serve as a pen. Most of the wall was intact, but parts had fallen into disrepair over the previous year. When Severus pushed a cartful of stones up and down the length of the wall, Genevieve would take the stones from the cart and position them while Gerontia, carrying the mortar bucket, spooned in cement with a trowel. The family worked in silence while the wind bit at their ears and fingers.

By afternoon, the wall was repaired, and the sheep were nestled in their piney shelters. Gerontia had begun lugging sacks of alfalfa up from the family's run-down barn to feed the sheep. Meanwhile, Severus handed Genevieve a sack of coins.

"Do you know the farmstead of Sabinianus? I need you to take this to him. It's payment for the alfalfa. He was kind enough to sell it to me on credit."

"Yes, of course, I know the way," replied Genevieve.

"Stay off the road," Severus said sternly. "Take the goat path along the tree line until you hit the creek, then go north across the field until you reach the farmstead."

"Yes, Papa, I know. I'll be home for dinner!"

And with that, the girl darted off, leaving her parents to the alfalfa. Her little legs carried her swiftly over crackled leaves and pine needles as she ran along the tree line. She'd been aching for another adventure since the day out with her father, and though running to a neighbor's farm was nothing special, it was at least *something*. And it was nice to get away from the sheep for a bit.

The goat path was a tiny footpath that ran along Valérien's lower slopes. It gave one a commanding view of the road and the Seine while providing a good deal of cover from the bushes and brambles that dotted the hillside. She looked down on the road as she walked, remembering the soldiers she had seen there a few days ago.

I wonder if there will be more soon.

It only took a half hour to round the base of Mont Valérien. The path then split from the mountain and ran down into a meadow crossed by a little creek that meandered through the fields. Genevieve took a running start and leapt over the creek. She cleared the water but slipped and fell on her face on the opposite bank, tumbling into the snow-dusted grass. She rose quickly and brushed herself off, but her tunic was stained with dirt. This would frustrate some mothers, but hers was used to her daughter coming home dirty.

It was another twenty minutes to the farmstead of Sabinianus, a shabby old construction of crumbling plaster with faded, broken tiles on the roof. It must have been a grand villa once, but it was well past its prime. Now the hulking structure looked haunted, sitting alone in the midst of a dreary field. Genevieve was not worried, though. She knew

Sabinianus and his family well. Her father had been purchasing feed from them for years, and Sabinianus likewise purchased wool from Severus—whatever was left over after the Duke took his share, that is.

Genevieve delivered the money dutifully and began her return journey. But by now, the snow was falling more heavily. Genevieve groaned at the thought of trudging back across the empty field and following the goat path in this weather. Instead, she started going another direction, toward the road.

I know what Papa said, but nobody will be out on an afternoon like this. I'm sure it's safe.

Having settled the matter with her conscience, and without much trouble, she bounded off toward the gravel lane.

The sky was a dull gray, thick with clouds, dumping snow in the surrounding fields, blanketing the once brown grasses in white. It was a wet kind of snow with large flakes that seemed to hang in the air. Genevieve trudged along contentedly, catching them on her tongue as she walked.

The land was quiet. Only the crunch of the snow beneath her feet could be heard. There was something beautiful about all of it, even purifying. It reminded her of a Scripture passage, but she couldn't recall which one. "Oh, my, what was it?" she said to herself. "As the snow falls . . . as the cold . . . hmm . . ." The passage eluded her.

Genevieve's thoughts were interrupted by the sound of hooves coming up the road. She stopped, straining to make sure her ears had not deceived her. No, it was surely the sound of horses, and more than one! She scrambled off the road and hid in the bushes just as she had with her father.

The horses came into sight not ten seconds later. It was only two riders, both men draped in long, fur-rimmed cloaks with hoods pulled over their heads.

They're not soldiers. And barbarians don't wear nice cloaks like those. Who are they?

The horsemen paused on the road near Genevieve's hiding spot.

No, don't stop! Keep going, keep going!

"Are you sure we've not become lost?" said one rider to his companion.

"I would have thought we'd see some sign of Paris by now," said the other, an older man with a silver beard. "By my reckoning, we should have approached it this morning."

Genevieve nodded, even though they couldn't see her, knowing they were way off course. The road they were presently on went through Nanterre, *away* from Paris. They had missed their turn some ways back.

"The way this snow is falling, we will be in a bad place by nightfall if we've gone astray," said the first.

"Should we continue or turn around?" asked the bearded man.

I can help them. I can tell them the right way! Or bring them to Nanterre so they can rest safely tonight.

Her father's warning interrupted her thoughts.

"Stay off the road," he had said. "That road is no place for an eight-year-old girl."

Genevieve knew nothing about these travelers, whether they were friend or foe. Were they brigands? Assassins? Perhaps it was best to stay out of sight.

But wait. Jesus said we're supposed to help people in need, right? I can't just let them wander out in the snow. They don't even know where they are.

"Say there, look at that!" said one of the men. Genevieve gasped. He was pointing at her own fresh footprints that led from the road to her hiding spot. As she crawled back, intending to flee, she rustled nearby bushes.

"In the name of Christ, show yourself," the bearded man thundered.

Genevieve pressed her body to the snowy earth and held still.

"Come out, we know you're there," the man called again.

Genevieve stood up and meekly stepped forward, trembling with head downcast.

"Ah, Germanus, it's just some local urchin," said the other. "Let's move on."

"Wait, Lupus. Maybe she can help. What is your name, girl?"

"I am called Genevieve, sir," she answered timidly.

"Heavens, she's terrified," said the bearded man. "Girl, have no fear. We are Christian men, clerics both. I am Germanus, Bishop of Auxerre. My companion is Lupus, Bishop of Troyes. We mean you no harm."

"Bishops!" Genevieve immediately dropped to her knees in the snow with hands folded.

"Girl, have you never seen a bishop before?" asked Lupus.

"No, sir," she said, looking at the ground. "I've heard of them but never seen nor spoken to one."

"Arise, Genevieve," ordered Germanus, lowering his hood to reveal a wizened old face with friendly eyes. "You may be of help to us. Tell me, are we nearing Paris?"

She shook her head as she rose to her feet. "No, you are on the wrong road. This road goes to Nanterre and then west."

"I knew it!" said Lupus. "We should have turned at the crossroads."

"It's too far to turn back today," said Germanus. "Genevieve, we are not from these parts. Can you tell us what sort of town is Nanterre? May we find lodging there?"

"It is only a village, sir. But we have a church where I'm sure you will be welcome. We are all Christian people."

"Who is your priest?" asked Lupus.

"We have no priest," said the girl. "We haven't for some time. Just a deacon. Our priest was killed."

"I see," said Germanus, stroking his beard and looking up at the sky which turned darker by the minute. When he brought his gaze back down, he said, "I think Nanterre is our best option for now. Genevieve, would you like to ride on to Nanterre with us?"

"Yes, sir," she said, nodding. Lupus dismounted and took Genevieve by the hand, lifting her onto the back of Germanus's steed.

"Hang on back there," warned Germanus. Genevieve nodded, wrapping her arms around the bishop's back and burying her cold face in the folds of his cloak. Lupus mounted, and the party rode off toward Nanterre.

Genevieve had never ridden anything but a donkey, which was nothing like sitting on the back of this mighty horse. As she jostled around behind Germanus, she was still scared, or at least nervous, but not like before. The fear of the unknown—of who these men were and what their intentions might be—had faded. There was something in Germanus's face that was trustworthy. He had a kind countenance, the sort of face one implicitly trusted. And yet there was still the matter of her disobedience. There was no hiding it now. Papa would know. She hoped the excitement of the bishops' arrival would distract him from any sort of punishment he might bring down upon her.

Before long, they were in sight of the town, its stone homes huddled together with wisps of smoke curling up into the winter air. "Just as Genevieve said!" exclaimed Germanus. "I give thanks to God that on this snowy day he brought us a messenger, our little angel Genevieve, to guide us here."

"As the cold of snow in the time of harvest, so is a faithful messenger," added Lupus.

"Hey!" Genevieve blurted out. "What is that from?"

"It's from the Scriptures, child," answered Lupus. "The Old Testament book of Proverbs."

"That's the passage I was trying to remember earlier!"

"Are you familiar with the Sacred Scriptures?" Germanus asked, turning his head back toward her.

Genevieve hesitated. "Somewhat. My mom has taught me all the basic Christian prayers. We went to Mass when we had a priest. Since he died, we've been attending vespers. I can read some, and Deacon Mucianus gave me a little scroll that contains lovely passages, the sayings of Christ, Psalms, Proverbs. I know the Proverbs fairly well."

"Can you tell me one?" said Lupus.

"A Proverb?" The girl cleared her throat. "The horse is prepared for the day of battle, but victory belongs to the Lord."

"That's an odd Proverb for a little girl to know! What do girls know of battle?"

Germanus chuckled. "Even if she will never see physical battle, Lupus, every Christian wages a spiritual battle for their soul."

"I want to see a battle!" Genevieve said.

"Keep living in these parts, and chances are you will," mumbled Lupus.

"Hush!" scolded Germanus. "We don't want to frighten the girl."

After a moment riding in silence, Genevieve said, "My house is nearby. If you wait here, I will fetch my father."

The two bishops agreed, allowing Genevieve to dismount the horse and run up the road toward her homestead, almost stumbling from excitement.

A half hour later, Genevieve returned with her parents, who escorted Germanus and Lupus into Nanterre. The arrival of the bishops caused quite a stir. As Genevieve had hoped, their arrival overshadowed her disobedience. Severus even beamed with pride as Germanus heaped praise upon the girl: "A fine girl you have there. We are very fortunate we found her on the road! If it weren't for her, we may not have come to Nanterre! And she's incredibly bright, too!"

The whole town turned out to see the bishops. There was no room for them in Genevieve's house, so they gathered that evening in a neighbor's hay barn. Genevieve soon realized that this Germanus was a man of some reputation. The villagers fawned over him like he was royalty. Men of the village—hardy men, rugged and scarred from the challenges of peasant life—threw themselves on their knees like children in the presence of the bishop, asking for his blessing.

"Mama, why is Germanus so important?"

"Well, that's an interesting story," said Gerontia, settling into a pile of hay, her daughter on her lap. "Germanus used to be a duke. He even knew Emperor Honorius."

Genevieve looked at the silver-bearded bishop smiling and laying his hands on the heads of those who crowded about him for a blessing. "*He* used to be a duke?"

"Yes, and a very powerful one. He was haughty, given to feasting and the hunt. Very worldly. But he was rebuked by a holy man, Saint Amator, and converted, reforming his life."

"And he wanted to be a bishop?" asked Genevieve.

"Not exactly," laughed Gerontia. "The people of Auxerre surrounded him and demanded him for their bishop. He took it to be the will of God and allowed himself to be consecrated. And it's a good thing he did! He is a very good and holy man. One of the greatest bishops of Gaul."

Genevieve looked at Germanus with newfound respect. She struggled to believe that she had ridden on a horse with a man who had known both the emperor and a saint. The simple horse ride was the most important thing that had ever happened to her!

Gradually, the excitement died down, and people seated themselves in the hay. Genevieve and her mother were tucked in the corner with other village women, while Severus leaned against the wall nearby with some of the townsmen. Everyone seemed eager to hear what Severus and Lupus would say.

"People of Nanterre," Severus began, standing in the midst of them, "my brother bishop Lupus and I are humbled by your generosity toward us. Though we cannot possibly repay your kindness, we want to do something to help you. We have heard how for some time you have been deprived of a priest, relying entirely on your deacon, the good Mucianus. Tomorrow, therefore, we will say Holy Mass in your church and administer Holy Communion to those who are disposed."

There were sighs of relief and murmurs of excitement. Most had not received Communion for nine months.

Deacon Mucianus stood up. "Good bishops, we have suffered much this year with no priest. We have made our situation known to the Bishop of Paris, but thus far he has not relieved us. In your mercy, can you speak to the Bishop of Paris for us? Or if not, send us a priest of your own choosing?"

"We will be calling on Bishop Marcellus when we visit Paris," said Lupus. "We will surely bring this matter before him. Hopefully, the Lord will move him to send someone to you."

"And why have you come?" called out Severus. "We are a long way from Auxerre and Troyes. What is your business?"

The two men looked at one another, seeming to wish the other to answer. Germanus obliged. "There is a dreadful heresy spreading in the west. It is called Pelagianism, from the

British priest Pelagius. The Gallic bishops have selected Lupus and me to travel to Britain to combat this vile teaching."

"We are supposed to meet other members of our group in Paris before crossing over to Britain," added Lupus. "But by accident, we ended up here instead."

"Thank God you did," grunted one of the villagers. "The western lands between here and Britain are swarming with Franks. You don't want to run into them. Filthy pagans, they are!"

"Aye," called another villager, a grizzled old fellow. "You're just as likely to wind up with an ax in your skull. Look at this!" He pointed to his face, drawing attention to a long, hideous scar running from his forehead down to his mouth. "I was lucky to escape with my life. Would have been killed, except the Frank that done it to me was too drunk to get a solid shot."

"We are aware of the dangers," said Germanus calmly. "Every day, the barbarian hordes increase, pushing further into Roman territory. God knows what the end of it all will be. But that does not change our resolve. There are Christian folk in the west being led astray by the errors of Pelagius, and the bishops of Gaul have chosen us to go unto them. This we will do, with God's grace."

"I've not heard much about this new heresy," said Mucianus. "What does this Pelagius teach?"

"It is a damnable heresy," said Lupus. "It has to do with the grace of God. We Catholics say that our salvation is made possible by the grace that Our Lord Jesus Christ won on the cross"—he bowed at the name of Christ—"but the Pelagians say Christ merited no grace for us. Rather, they say He saves us by providing us a good example to imitate, and this is the whole of it. Now, there is *some* truth to what the Pelagians say because, of course, we are to imitate Our Lord. But I think it really comes down to the question of what grace is and how it affects us. For example . . ."

Lupus and Germanus launched into an explanation of the differences between Pelagian and Catholic teachings about grace, which Genevieve found too difficult to understand. Even so, she liked hearing the bishop speak. People in Nanterre seldom spoke about anything save for fish, sheep, and farming. She loved hearing words like *efficacious*, *merited*, and *salvific*, terms she didn't understand but which flowed from the lips of the bishops like honey. It made her feel like part of the adult world.

Her eyes suddenly began to feel heavy. She cuddled up in Gerontia's lap so that her mother could wrap her wiry arms around the girl. Genevieve looked about the barn, at all the familiar faces flickering in the torchlight, listening intently to the bishops' teachings. Genevieve so seldom saw all the village together like this—not these days, anyway.

With these thoughts, she drifted off to sleep in her mother's arms.

Chapter 3

The Words Are Inside of Me

Genevieve stretched her dirty, soot-covered toes from under her bedcovering and inched them closer to the dying embers. Pulling her wool blanket tightly around her, she took in the final gasps of heat from last night's fire. A few candles burned in the corner, throwing golden light on the little scroll she studied in her hands. She squinted at the dark characters on the page. "Let the children come to me," she murmured. "Do not hinder them, for to such belong the kingdom of heaven."

Her mother sat up on the straw mattress in the corner. "What are you doing up so early, Genevieve?" she asked in a groggy voice.

"Practicing these verses," the girl answered quietly.

"Ah, still looking at that scroll Mucianus gave you?" Gerontia smiled. She slipped quietly out from under the blankets to sit beside Genevieve, leaving Severus slumbering alone. She grabbed kindling from a rusted old bucket nearby and threw it on the embers. "Is this your way of preparing for Mass today?"

"Yes," nodded Genevieve. "It's been so long since we've been to Mass, I wanted to make it more special."

"My good girl," her mother said, running her hand through Genevieve's long blond hair. "I'm very proud of you leading Germanus and Lupus here."

"I was worried Papa would be mad at me for going on the road when he told me not to."

"You got caught in a snowfall, and you made the best decision you could with the knowledge you had. And you met two remarkable people on the road, and now because of you, our town is having Mass for the first time in nine months. I think God used you, Genevieve."

The girl said nothing, continuing to pore over the scroll. But her mother's words startled her. God was using her?

Why would God use me? I'm just an eight-year-old girl. Aren't there more important people in the world He'd rather use?

Her eyes wandered again over the text of the scroll. "Let the children come to me . . ."

Mother and daughter sat on the sooty floor beside the fireplace for some time, enjoying the morning silence. As the darkness gave way to the dim of morning, Severus roused himself, grumbled, and put on his trousers. Gerontia, too, began preparing for the day. The fire now crackling, she hung a kettle over the flames to heat some water. "Genevieve, please go check the sheep. Germanus announced Mass will be midmorning. We need to have at least some of our chores done by then."

"Yes, Mama."

Genevieve pulled her stockings up over her grimy feet, strapped on her boots, and pulled two cloaks over her head to keep the cold out. She rolled up the scroll and tucked it away in her sleeve, hoping to read more on the way to the sheep pen.

The morning was gray, and a chill hung over the land. There was no snowfall or heavy wind, and the previous days' snow upon the ground had a sparkly sheen like a dusting of crystals shining on the fields and rooftops. The first light was spilling over the horizon. Yesterday's snowfall had settled in some, and the grass peeked through, stiff and crackling under Genevieve's feet. The whole world had a crisp feeling about it. She exhaled strongly, delighted at the sight of her breath wafting in the air like smoke.

She studied the scroll more while walking across the fields to the pen. "I think there was something in here about sheep," she said to herself, scanning the sheet. "Ah, here it is . . . 'My sheep know my voice, and I know them, and they follow me.'" She mouthed the passage several more times, pondering what it meant.

How am I like a sheep?

The sheep—the real sheep—were huddled together in the trees but roused themselves with eager bleating when they saw Genevieve approach. She stuffed the scroll into her tunic, took up a wooden pitchfork, and began bailing alfalfa over the stone wall and into the pen. The sheep crowded around, jostling and crunching up the alfalfa as she bailed. She worked quickly, not wanting to make her family late for Germanus's liturgy.

When the sheep were fed, Genevieve trotted off back toward the homestead. She reached for her scroll to read from it more, but it was not in her tunic. She stopped, panic creeping in. She patted all over, searching unsuccessfully. It was gone! Genevieve retraced her steps to the sheep pen, scanning the ground like an eagle for the scroll. Finding nothing, she returned to the enclosure to look there. Perhaps it had fallen out while she bailed alfalfa?

Genevieve gasped when she saw the shreds sticking out of a sheep's mouth as he munched.

"No!" She leapt over the wall. "You silly sheep! Open your mouth this instant!"

She tried to pry the scroll from its teeth, but her little hands were too weak, and the sheep was not intimidated.

"I'm going to have you for dinner!" she cried, beating her fists against its thick woolen hide. Tears began to sting her eyes. But echoing her father's threats proved just as fruitless. The animal munched on, oblivious to the girl's pain or the importance of its snack.

She trudged back to the house in tears, clutching in her fists the few fragments of Mucianus's scroll she had managed to tear from the sheep's mouth. Her mother and father were too preoccupied with preparing for Mass to notice Genevieve's distress. But she did not want it on display anyhow, and drying her eyes and sniffles, she marched off with her parents into Nanterre.

The church of Nanterre was an old stone structure dating back a hundred years. It was dedicated to a child-martyr named Saint Justin, about whom Genevieve knew little. Supposedly, he was buried under the altar, but she did not know if this was true. Another supposed connection he had to the town was the claim by the villagers that fruits and vegetables picked on his feast day—August 1—were especially wholesome, even capable of warding off illnesses. Again, Genevieve could not verify this, but she knew Justin was holy if he was a saint who died for Christ.

The church had narrow arched windows lining both sides, and its roof was shingled with slate, though the slate was in disarray in some places, a testimony to the poverty of Nanterre. The most distinctive feature of the church was the bell tower protruding up from the apse. Square and plain, the tower reached thirty feet, making it the tallest structure in town.

"When I was a lad, there used to be monks living here," Severus said, pointing up toward the tower. "They used to ring the bell seven times a day."

The tower being closed as it was, Genevieve could see no bell. "Is it still there?" she asked.

"No," her father grunted. He looked dejected. Genevieve turned to her mother.

"The town had to melt it down to pay a ransom to the Goths sometime before you were born," she said.

The townsfolk filed dutifully through the church's arched doors. Though this was the first Mass in quite some time, Genevieve came here often to pray vespers with Deacon Mucianus or for baptisms or merely as a meeting place with other villagers. Her father conducted plenty of business "at the portal," as the villagers said when they wanted to meet at the church doors. Genevieve happily tagged along, dipping inside the church for prayer or just to sit in silence while her father chatted with locals in the street. The interior was usually gray and shadowy, but today the altar was brightened by many candles, no doubt pulled from Mucianus's reserves.

The villagers stood about on the flagstone floor, though a few elderly folks brought stools to sit on. When Germanus, Lupus, and Mucianus processed to the altar, chanting a sonorous Latin hymn, it signaled the beginning of the liturgy. Genevieve could not understand the words of the hymn, but many of the adults seemed to know it well enough to sing or at least hum along. Germanus, donned in flowing white vestments, bowed and kissed the altar, while Lupus, acting as a server, swung a censer, filling the air with thick, savory smoke. Genevieve closed her eyes and sniffed, taking in the rich scent that filled her heart with warmth. It had been so long since she smelled incense.

Mucianus turned to face the people. "*Tace! Audi!*" he chanted, meaning, "Be silent, listen!" The people dropped their heads in prayer, hands folded meekly.

"*Dóminus sit semper vobíscum,*" said Germanus, proclaiming the ancient greeting that the Lord would be with each and every person there.

"*Et cum spíritu tuo,*" the congregation replied.

Then followed a series of prayers: the Sanctus, the Kyrie, and the chanting of the Canticle of Zechariah.

"*Lectio prophetica!*" Mucianus bellowed, announcing the first reading from the prophets.

Germanus unfurled a massive, ancient scroll and read from it in the same booming voice with which he had first addressed Genevieve on the road. It was a reading from the Prophet Jeremiah. "'I know the plans I have for you,' declares the Lord, 'plans to prosper you and not to harm you, plans to give you a future and a hope.'"

What does it mean to hope? Genevieve thought.

She looked down at the tattered fragments of Mucianus's scroll resting in her palm. Then looking up, she noticed the faces around her in the church, those who were downcast, sad, worn down by the trials of life. Talk of hope seemed to depress them rather than enliven them, her father included. Yet others seemed uplifted, aglow with happiness at hearing the reading, as if they had already taken hold of the hope the prophet spoke of. Her mother's face seemed to reflect this hope.

The Gospel reading that followed was a frightening passage from Matthew that Genevieve was unfamiliar with. It spoke of cities being surrounded and abominations and desolations and people fleeing into the cold wilderness. It was disquieting. The images alarmed Genevieve; the adults, too, shifted uncomfortably as the scriptural promises of impending doom were pronounced authoritatively by Bishop Germanus. With all the tumults occurring in the world, it was no stretch for the people of Nanterre to apply the judgments mentioned by Christ to their own day.

When it came time for Germanus's sermon, he preached on the importance of clinging to Christ during difficult times. Genevieve could now understand why this man was so venerated. Listening to him speak was like honey for the soul. He spoke of the Church as a ship in the midst of a terrifying storm and Jesus Christ as the great captain. Upon this ship, the cross of Our Lord was like the mast, to which all must be attentive to and cling to in storm-tossed waves. It filled Genevieve with a sense of bold confidence in the goodness of God, regardless of what came to pass.

After the homily, Germanus chanted a litany from the ambo, invoking the Holy Trinity under various titles in preparation for the Offertory. But as he chanted, the bishop suddenly paused as if struck dumb. His eyes glazed over. The congregation shuffled and murmured uncomfortably, looking around, whispering. Mucianus stood awkwardly with hands folded, uncertain whether this sudden silence was a usual part of Germanus's Masses.

Lupus elbowed the bishop. "Germanus! Are you all right?"

Germanus suddenly came to and resumed chanting the litany as if he'd never stopped.

The rest of the Mass proceeded in a usual manner. Prior to Communion, Germanus turned to the people, made a prayer of considerable length, and gave his blessing. "May the peace, faith, and charity and communion in the body and blood of Our Lord be with you always," he said, making the sign of the cross over the congregation.

Genevieve felt particularly devout receiving Holy Communion. She realized how deeply she had missed this during the past nine months—and she worried about when she would have another chance.

Lord, if you send a priest to Nanterre, I promise I won't take it for granted. I will attend Mass and receive you as often as I can.

"May the Body and Blood of Our Lord Jesus Christ preserve thy soul unto life eternal," said Germanus as he reverently placed the Sacred Host upon the girl's tongue. Her mother and father received the sacrament as well, each making the sign of the cross as they knelt before the successor of the Apostles.

After Mass, the villagers milled about, hoping to have more time with the bishops. Germanus, however, seemed distracted. He blessed the people and greeted them with his characteristic kindness, but it was clear that though he was there physically, mentally he was absent.

Catching sight of Genevieve's family, his eyes widened as if he'd been looking for them. "Severus! Gerontia!" he called. "Lupus and I must be on our way soon, but may we call on you before we go?"

"Of course," said Severus, bowing his head. "The honor is ours."

Later as the family walked home, Gerontia asked, "What do they want?"

Her husband shrugged. "Probably just to express their gratitude. Nothing to be concerned about."

"One of the most renowned bishops asks to come over, and you say it's nothing to be concerned about?" quipped Gerontia. The two bickered on, but Genevieve's mind was elsewhere. Her chest felt warm despite the cold weather, as if something were glowing inside her. Her heart raced. She glanced down to her hand and the fragments of the scroll. She opened one of the tiny, torn pieces. "You are the light of the world," it read.

The family had not long been home when Germanus and Lupus arrived, along with the deacon Mucianus. Germanus immediately entered the home, pulled up a stool, and to everyone's amazement, addressed Genevieve before greeting her parents. "Genevieve," he said gravely, "did anything happen to you at Mass today?"

The girl thought for a moment. "I liked your sermon very much. And I was pleased to receive the Body of Our Lord."

"Yes, but did anything . . . *happen*?" The bishop stared at the girl intently.

"What is this about, Germanus?" asked Lupus.

"Yes, what are you getting at here?" Severus demanded, forgetting momentarily he was addressing a bishop.

"Well," Genevieve said meekly, "after I received Holy Communion, I felt something inside of me."

"Felt what?" her mother asked, stepping closer.

The girl shrugged. "Warmth I suppose is the best way to describe it."

"Can you explain it to me?" said the bishop.

The girl furled her brow and thought for a moment. "Remember the scroll I told you about? That I practiced reading the Scriptures from?"

"Yes."

"Before Mass, I was reading from it, and . . . I accidentally dropped it in the sheep pen. And the sheep ate it. All that is left are these few fragments." She held up the pieces and turned to Deacon Mucianus. "I'm sorry deacon! I didn't mean to!"

"Go on," said Germanus.

"Well, I was upset. I'd just decided I wanted to study more and learn the Scriptures better. Then I messed up. But after

Communion, I felt a burning fire in my breast. Like . . . like the words weren't truly gone. Like the words were . . . *inside* me."

Germanus leaned back and clapped his hands in childlike delight. A friendly smile beamed across his wrinkled face. "My dear Genevieve, it is not only your own heart that is warmed, but you warm the heart of this old bishop as well. Now, I will tell you something: During Mass, I was praying the litany after the homily when I was struck by something. Looking out at the people, I saw something—you, Genevieve, had a glowing light above your head. And I foresaw that you will be a woman of great holiness, a light to the people here. The light was so beautiful, I was lost in it until good Lupus roused me."

Genevieve's eyes widened. She opened her hand and looked again at the torn fragment in her palm. "You are the light of the world," it said. Her lip quivered, and she began to cry.

"That's enough! You're overwhelming the girl!" said Severus.

"No, Papa, I'm fine," said Genevieve, brushing away her tears. "What Germanus is saying makes me very happy."

"Genevieve," the bishop said delicately, "would you like to consecrate yourself to God as a holy virgin?"

"Yes!" she blurted out. "Yes! I want it more than anything!"

"Surely, she is too young to take vows!" Gerontia protested.

"Yes, of course she is," Germanus replied calmly. "She still must grow and discern. But if Genevieve persists in this desire and demonstrates the capacity for consecrated life, do you have any objections?"

Severus and Gerontia looked at one another, their faces filled with a mix of admiration and fear. "No," mumbled Severus. "If you think she has a vocation, it is an honor."

"I believe she does," replied the bishop. "Can you meet me in the church tomorrow before we depart? I will bless her there."

The parents agreed and the men departed.

Genevieve spent the rest of the morning wandering the hills behind her homestead deep in thought, looking into the pale blue sky. When she returned home, she cuddled up on her father's lap before the fire. He held her and said nothing, stroking her hair with his strong hands.

That evening, there was a discussion about practical matters. It was agreed that Genevieve would remain at home with her family until she was at least fifteen, at which point she would be permitted to make vows if she still wished to persist in her resolution.

The following morning, the family went to the church as planned. Germanus, Lupus, and Mucianus were there, along with several of the more devout townspeople. All present kneeled in prayer. After this, Germanus placed his hand on Genevieve's head and asked her if she would promise to be faithful to God.

"By His help, I will," she answered.

Germanus held up a bronze medallion with a cross engraved upon it, then fastened it around the girl's neck. "You are too young to take vows," he said, "but this medal will remind you of your promise to God. Let this be your only adornment. Do not wear bracelets or earrings or jewelry of vanity; glory only in the cross of Jesus Christ from now on."

She nodded, too overcome with emotion to respond.

Germanus then encouraged her parents before everyone to bring Genevieve up in a manner befitting a bride of Christ. Severus and Gerontia nodded and promised they would do so.

"As for the rest of you," Germanus said, "I give this command also: take care of this girl, watch over her, and be good to her. Nanterre is poor in the eyes of the world, but here in this girl is your treasure. Protect her. The Lord will bless you for her sake."

The villagers, too, agreed to their sacred charge.

When the ceremony was over, Germanus bade farewell to Genevieve and her family. "I want you to know I have prayed about the situation with your town. I am going to send you one of my own priests to minister here. He is a very good and holy man. He is training to be a missionary, but I think this assignment will be good for him and for you. Nanterre will again have a priest."

"But what about the Bishop of Paris?" asked Mucianus.

"I will smooth things over with him, good deacon," said Germanus reassuringly.

The deacon bowed humbly. "We are all indebted to you."

"Think nothing of it! Only promise that you, too, will keep an eye on Genevieve," the bishop said, grasping the deacon by the shoulder.

"As the Lord lives, it shall be so," promised Mucianus.

Just then, Lupus appeared at the church door, the bridles of the bishops' horses in his hands. "Well, shall we finally get on to Paris?"

Chapter 4

If Only Life Were Always Such as This

Germanus had called Genevieve the treasure of Nanterre. This title would have tempted most girls to vanity, but not Genevieve. On the contrary, in the passing years, she grew into a model of humility and grace. Ever cheerful, she was simple in appearance but resplendent in the adornments of virtue. The young girl was a blessing to all who knew her.

The villagers were faithful to the sacred charge Germanus had given them. They referred to her as "our Genevieve" and were quick to lend their aid to her family. Occasional visitors dropped by the homestead with gifts of bread or meat, wishing the family well and asking for Genevieve's prayers. At Christmas, some village women dropped by with new linen garments for the family, which were desperately needed. Sabinianus even sent over a complimentary cart of alfalfa for the sheep. Despite all this adoration, Severus and Gerontia did not become proud or overbearing. On the contrary, they regarded it all as a grace. They were profoundly thankful and always made it clear that they were undeserving of such attention.

After the feast of the Epiphany, the priest promised by Germanus showed up, a handsome, educated young man with a strange accent. His name was Patricius. Just like that, regular Masses were restored at Saint Justin's Church after an interval of a year. Patricius proved an energetic pastor, preaching with zeal and organizing a collection for the widows and the poor of Nanterre. His wholesome manner of living attracted several other local youths who were considering priesthood or religious life. He even managed to secure a donation from Duke Victorinus to repair the roof of Saint Justin's, giving the work to local men and ensuring the money would stay in the community.

Patricius also made it a point to visit the farmsteads of his parish and make himself known to each family. It was not long before he called on Genevieve's family to see the girl Germanus had told him about. One day, when the chill of winter was on the way out, late in the season of Lent, he found her pasturing her family's flocks in the sloping fields of Valérien.

"Hello, Genevieve," he said, strolling into the sheep pen.

Genevieve flipped around, startled.

"I'm sorry, I didn't mean to sneak up on you like that."

"No, it is fine."

"I am Patricius, the priest."

Genevieve giggled. "I know you are, Father! Everyone in town knows you."

Patricius smiled. "I guess you're right. Still, it's nice to make a proper introduction." He looked about the farmstead and took a deep breath through his nose. "Ah, spring is always a nice time to be a shepherd. The green grasses start to peek up from the snow again. The sun starts to warm you a bit, and it isn't so bad being outside like in the winter."

"Have you kept sheep before, Father?" the young girl asked, the two of them starting to walk along the stone wall that bounded her family's field.

"Aye," said Patricius. "I was a slave when I was a young man. My master had me keep sheep on his mountainside, not unlike your Mont-Valérien here—but with fewer trees."

"*You* were a slave? Were you . . . born a slave? Where were you enslaved? How . . . how did you gain your freedom? And how did you meet Germanus?"

Patricius laughed. "What a curious one you are!"

Genevieve hung her head. "I'm sorry, Father. I shouldn't pry."

"No, no, it's all right. Children your age are supposed to be curious. I was not born a slave; I was captured and forced into slavery in a place called Ireland. Eventually, I escaped and came to Gaul. I found my way to Auxerre and met the good bishop Germanus. It is he who ordained me to the priesthood."

"How did you escape slavery?" Genevieve asked, her eyes wide.

"I'm afraid that will have to be a story for another time. It's quite long and complicated, and that's not why I came to see you today. I came to see you, Genevieve, to give you a little advice."

The girl looked up at him as they walked.

"Make sure you use this time for preparation," he said.

When he didn't go on, she said, "I'm afraid I don't know what you mean, Father."

He pulled his eyes down to her. "Moses was eighty years old before God used him to deliver the Israelites from Egypt. Did you know that?" Genevieve shook her head. "And before Saint Paul began his preaching, he spent three years in solitude in Arabia."

"I did not know that either," Genevieve said, somewhat embarrassed.

"You will learn much more about the Scriptures as you get older. The point is that you cannot take the veil until you get older. You have a few more years at home still, and you should use this time wisely. Prepare yourself for what God will use you for."

"But I don't know what God will use me for."

"Do not concern yourself with that," the priest said calmly. "He knows what plans He has for you. That's all that matters. You must simply offer your life to Him, and He will use you as His providence sees fit. For now, pray, pray very much, and prepare yourself for your vocation."

Genevieve thought for a moment. "How did you prepare before you came to Gaul and became a priest?"

Patricius smiled and looked off wistfully toward Mont-Valérien. "I was always outside on the mountain, always exposed to the weather, seldom able to go into town to speak with anyone. I devoted my time to prayer. I would make a little cross of wood, stick it into the ground, and kneel in front of it."

"How often did you do that?"

"A hundred times a day, a hundred times a night," said Patricius, still looking at the wooded slopes of Mont-Valérien. His mind seemed elsewhere, lost in distant memory, as if he missed it.

"*That* often?" Genevieve exclaimed.

Patricius finally looked back at her. "Well, maybe I've picked up a wee bit of the Irish love for exaggeration," he said with a wink. "But I prayed a lot."

"I see," said Genevieve. "Thank you, Father. I will take your advice."

"Good girl," said the priest, tussling Genevieve's mop of blond hair. "Who knows what journeys God may have in store for you—or for me!"

The priest imparted his blessing to the girl, hopped over the stone wall, and continued up the road to call on the other homesteads outside of town. He turned and waved to Genevieve before passing out of sight.

Genevieve wasted little time taking Patricius's advice to heart. Finding a secluded grove in the trees upon the slope, the girl fashioned a cross of sticks, lashed them together with twine, and tied it to one of the tree trunks. There she knelt on the damp ground, hands folded, eyes fixed on the cross. She did not know what to say, so she just stared. She felt the crisp, March breeze on her face and listened to the noises of the sheep grazing lazily about her. The only prayer she made, uttered in the silence of her heart, was, *"Jesus, help me."*

Genevieve passed many hours thereafter in her little oratory in the trees. As the weather turned warm and the trees bloomed, her grove became a den of green foliage. She christened the place her "Green Circle." Father Patricius was kind enough to give her a new scroll with some passages from the Prophet Isaiah. These, too, she brought to the Green Circle to practice.

Spring was the time for the shearing. Genevieve and her parents worked their hands raw for a week, cutting the wool off the sheep. Another two weeks was spent carding the wool, sorting through the vast piles and scraping them over with a heavy iron comb which straightened the wool, orienting the fibers in the same direction and allowing them to be organized by length. Severus and Gerontia did most of the carding, while Genevieve organized the combed wool into bundles, tied them off, and bagged them in linen sacks.

It was grueling work, but Genevieve enjoyed watching her father work the comb through the wool, his forearms bulging from the labor. Genevieve had tried carding last year and could only do it for twenty minutes before her arm got too stiff and tired. But Severus uttered no complaint. He combed relentlessly, head down, sweat beaded upon his brow, hour after hour, day after day, until the job was done. At first, Genevieve marveled at how different her father's rough peasant demeanor was from that of an educated man like Father Patricius. But then again, was the perseverance of her father pulling that comb a hundred times that much different from Father Patricius praying a hundred times a day? Fortitude was fortitude, equally admirable in priest and peasant.

When it came time for Easter, the town enjoyed a reprieve from the rigors of Lent and the labors of shearing. The church of Saint Justin was festive with its white altar cloths and drapery, the entire building festooned with flowers and garlands woven from ivy by the village girls. Genevieve had never seen the church so joyous as the people on Nanterre celebrated the resurrection of Christ by candlelight. For the rest of her days, Genevieve would never forget the face of Patricius, aglow by the light of the Paschal candle, as he intoned *Lumen Christi*—"Light of Christ!"—inaugurating the holiest Mass of the Christian Church.

The week after Easter, Duke Victorinus arrived to gather Nanterre's quotas for his army. Each family in the town had a quota to meet: wool, hay, linens, iron, rope—anything that could be produced for the benefit of the imperial cause was collected. The duke spent an entire day amassing his due.

When he came to Severus's farmstead on horseback in the company of several clerks and officials, Genevieve and her family lined up dutifully to greet him, bowing as his retinue approached. Duke Victorinus was an imposing man, tall, gruff, and draped in a cloak of gray. He was a model of Roman dignity as he sat atop his horse, saying nothing while the imperial clerks loaded the family's woolen sacks into carts, carefully recording each and paying a handful of silver coins per sack.

The duke, after a minute of looking passively around the landside, suddenly perked up when his eyes slid across

Genevieve. "Girl! You are the one they call Genevieve, are you not?"

Genevieve, keeping her eyes downcast, answered, "Yes, my lord."

The duke dismounted, his boots squishing in the soft, muddy earth. He trudged over to Genevieve and her mother, inspecting them. Severus watched nervously. The duke was all-powerful and could do whatever he wanted with whomever he wished. It was best to be ignored by such people, or so Severus thought.

"We've heard of you in Paris. The girl Germanus saw the light over," the duke said. "They say Nanterre will have its own saint one day. Are you a saint?"

Genevieve blushed. "I . . . I have never claimed any such thing," she stammered. Gerontia grasped Genevieve's hand and squeezed it.

Duke Victorinus could see the anxiety on the faces of Genevieve and her family. A dry smile slowly spread across his face. "Well, in case you are a saint, I've brought something for you," he said warmly. Throwing back his cloak, he rummaged about in a belt pouch and pulled out a ring of polished bronze with crosses crudely engraved in a circuit around the band. He took the girl's delicate hand into his massive, gloved palm, and with the other hand, slid the ring on her tiny finger.

"Ah! A perfect fit!" he said.

It actually was *not* a perfect fit—it was rather loose—but Genevieve thought it best not to complain.

"Thank you, my lord!" exclaimed Gerontia, bowing. "We are most grateful."

"That ring belonged to a consecrated virgin of Paris who died some years ago," Victorinus explained, still holding Genevieve's hand in his own. "It was handed over to me as part of an effort to raise money to equip our men to fight the Burgundians. But it seemed . . . not right . . . to melt it down, so I've held on to it. When I heard about you, I thought it might suit you. I heard you were a shepherd's daughter, but I wasn't sure I'd get the chance to meet you. I'm glad I did."

Genevieve shook her head. "I don't know what to say, my lord."

"Say nothing. Just pray for me."

Victorinus released her hand, turned, and stomped back to mount his horse, reassuming the dignified duke of imperial Rome. They were gone a few minutes later, a procession of horses and carts winding up the road to the next village.

That night, the family prayed for the fortunes of Duke Victorinus as they cuddled around the fireplace. Genevieve curled up in her mother's arms, looking at the ring and spinning it about on her finger.

Who wore this? What was her story? How did she die? How long ago?

So many questions which, unfortunately, would have to remain unanswered. Her mother recommended she keep the ring stored somewhere safe until she was big enough to wear it. Genevieve knew that was a prudent idea; she did not want to lose it in some alfalfa pile like the scroll of Mucianus.

The next several years of Genevieve's life were idyllic. The winters were mild and summers joyful. The harvests were plentiful, and Nanterre was spared any of the chaos unfolding in the world. Some years, Duke Victorinus sent officials to collect supplies on his behalf, but he returned one spring when Genevieve was twelve. He smiled and waved at Genevieve but said nothing. Although it had only been three years since the day he gave her the ring, his face looked considerably worn down.

Patricius sadly left Nanterre for a new assignment, but the Bishop of Paris sent another priest to replace him in short order, a young man called Quintilian. Masses, baptisms, marriages, and funerals went on as the liturgical feasts marked the passing of seasons. Genevieve spent many long hours in the church, mostly praying, but every now and then, old Deacon Mucianus allowed her to read from the New Testament codex he kept there. She was elated to have the chance to study the Scriptures and became even more excited when several other young girls from Nanterre, inspired by Genevieve's example, resolved to take the veil when they came of age. The girls formed a club, gathering in the church or in Genevieve's Green Circle to talk, pray, and read. For the first time, Genevieve felt like she had real friends. That they were united in the holy resolution of serving Christ as virgins only strengthened their bond.

When Genevieve turned fifteen, the family began preparing for her to take vows in Paris. The old bishop, Marcellus, had died, and there was a new bishop, a man called Vivianus. He had written to Mucianus and asked the deacon to bring the girls of Nanterre at Pentecost to take vows. Bishop

Vivianus, however, said the girls were too young to enter the convent. Given they had formed a little club in Nanterre, he directed the priest Quintilian and Deacon Mucianus to organize them into a small community, lodging them at the church so they could become at least somewhat familiar with religious life before heading into the convent in Paris. Genevieve was thrilled at the news. The thought of living at Saint Justin's with her companions for a few more years gave her great joy.

That June, when the wildflowers were bursting in the fields of Nanterre, Deacon Mucianus summoned the girls to accompany him to Paris. Severus bid Genevieve farewell at the corner of the farmstead, wrapping her in his thick arms beside the old stone wall.

"I'll be back soon, Papa," she said, burying her face in his chest.

"My brave girl," her father said, kissing her forehead.

Gerontia accompanied the little group to Paris to witness her daughter's vows. The sky was clear and blue, and the fields bore rich hues of green. The waters of the Seine shone like crystal in the sunlight. On the journey, which felt more like a procession, the girls sang and laughed and dreamed about what they hoped the future would hold. Gerontia smiled, watching her daughter with her friends. It filled her heart to see the girl so carefree. "If only life were always such as this," Gerontia said wistfully.

The party approached Paris by dusk. The girls marveled and pointed; none of them had ever seen a city so large, swelling out in crowded blocks around the Seine and enclosed by a wooden palisade. A detachment of imperial soldiers guarded the gates of the city, keeping a keen eye on the throngs of peasants, merchants, and officials who streamed in and out. Mucianus pointed to a tall stone spire protruding from the heart of the city. "There is the Church of Saint Etienne, the seat of the diocese. We will find Bishop Vivianus there."

They passed through the palisade and entered the city. It was both better and worse than Genevieve had imagined. She was not prepared for the sheer size of it. A single block in Paris was larger than all of Nanterre. The roads were thronged with hundreds of people from all walks of life, going about their business. Wood and stone buildings lined the streets more than Genevieve had ever seen in a single place. The bustle filled her with vibrant energy.

And yet she was not expecting Paris to be so dirty. The roads were concourses of mud, such that Genevieve's tunic quickly became stained to the knees. The air was also full of smoke from Paris's many homes and shops, stinging her eyes. And the animals! Herdsmen drove swine, geese, and goats through the streets while stray dogs roamed. The muddy streets were laced with animal droppings churned beneath the feet of the people passing through. The odor was almost too much for the small-town girls to bear.

Night had fallen by the time the group came to the Seine district, where the imperial officials' quarters were clustered along the riverside and where Duke Victorinus kept his residence—though, these days he was seldom there. Soldiers and court officials thronged the street along the Seine. Out on the river, a stone bridge connected the mainland to a narrow island. The island, too, was full of buildings, most notably a large stone church built in the old Roman style.

"Is that the bishop's church?" one of the girls asked.

"Yes," answered Mucianus. "That is Saint Etienne's, the seat of the Church of Paris. We will lodge there for the night."

The party crossed over the bridge to the church. The Seine was quiet, dotted with fishing boats illumined by lamps which cast gentle yellow light reflecting over the water. The bells of Saint Etienne's rung, announcing Compline. The first stars twinkled in the dark blue firmament. A warm breeze swirled off the river, dispelling the city's odors and kissing Genevieve.

"Finally," Gerontia said, "we've gotten away from the smell a bit. It's pleasant the way Saint Etienne's sits on the Seine, isn't it?"

"It's all so beautiful," Genevieve said to her mother.

"It is, in its own way," said Gerontia. "Paris has its charms."

CHAPTER 5

The Noose Tightens

The day Genevieve took her vows was like a dream. She had prepared for this moment for years, but it passed by so quickly. Kneeling with her companions in the morning before the altar of Saint Etienne's, Bishop Vivianus placed his hands on the head of each girl, prayed a simple prayer, and asked them if they swore, with God's help, to consecrate themselves as sacred virgins to the service of Christ and His Church.

"We do," they solemnly affirmed.

"Be thou consecrated unto God as befits true spouses of Jesus Christ," said Vivianus, making the sign of the cross over the girls. "First fruits unto God and the Lamb, who follow him wherever he goes."

"Amen," the girls said.

Deacon Mucianus stepped forward, holding a pair of shears. One by one, he sliced off the girls' hair at the shoulder, the ancient sign of religious consecration. Genevieve knelt with hands folded, eyes downcast, watching strands of her flaxen hair fall upon the flagstone as the old man cut it away. By the time he was done, all that was left was two singular tresses hanging down either side of her head, as was the Gallic custom.

Next, the newly consecrated were presented with veils made of undyed wool. These veils were meant to be a sign of their simplicity of life, but for a poor shepherd girl like Genevieve, it was scarcely different from the clothes she had always worn.

Following the consecration, Vivianus spoke with the group. "You are not yet old enough for monastic life. I have arranged for you to live in community under the supervision of Deacon Mucianus and the priest Quintilian. This will be a time of formation for you, a time to learn the sweet yoke of Christ, to grow in virtue as you learn to live in common. This period will last for two years. At the end of two years, you will join the community of virgins here in Paris."

Vivianus closed the ceremony by imparting his episcopal blessing. Afterward, Gerontia hugged her daughter. "I'm so proud of you," she said, beaming. Then taking Genevieve's hand, she slipped the bronze ring given by Duke Victorinus onto her finger. "I think it's fitting you should have this now."

Genevieve smiled as she looked down at the ring which now, all these years later, finally fit. "Thank you for coming with me, Mother," she said, kissing her mother's cheek.

The sky was blue and the sun radiant on the joyful journey back to Nanterre. On several occasions, the party was stopped by peasants asking for the girls' prayers, offering them gifts of food and drink. "My!" one of the girls marveled. "It's amazing the difference these veils make!"

The other girls giggled.

"The splendor of the veil is in the treasures of grace it makes available," said Genevieve, working her two remaining tresses into thick braids. "It is not the temporal gifts we receive."

The girls rolled their eyes. "Don't be so uptight," another said.

"Genevieve is right," said Mucianus. "Though I know your comment was innocent, you must not get used to an easy life. The life of a consecrated virgin is meant to be one of discipline and penance. Your lives are free from difficulty now, but when tribulation comes, how will you endure if you have only been accustomed to luxury? Remember, if anyone blesses you or makes a gift to you or honors you, it is on account of Christ whom you represent. Let all things be referred back to him."

The old man's rebuke soured conversation, leaving the girls to walk in silence. Mucianus was, of course, correct. And Genevieve and her companions would learn this sooner than later.

Back home, the girls lived in a small house attached to Saint Justin's that Quintilian had built. It was rustic, not much different from the other houses of Nanterre, but sufficient for the needs of the little community. The girls prayed the Divine Office with Quintilian and Mucianus every day, rising early for Lauds and retiring after Compline, sometimes even waking in the middle of the night for prayers as well. During the day, they kept busy with manual labor around the church or undertaking works of mercy in the town. They took their meals twice a day, usually a frugal dish of cooked vegetables and bread, often provided by a village family. On Sundays, they celebrated Mass with the rest of the town—though seated apart by themselves—and would occasionally take religious instruction from Quintilian or spend the rest of the Lord's Day visiting their families or reading in the Green Circle as they had done as girls. It was a beautiful life, and Genevieve was truly happy.

It was, however, the last happy year Genevieve would know for a long time. The year 436 was one of disaster. The *magister militum* of the West, Flavius Aetius, led a force of imperial troops and mercenaries in a massive battle against the Burgundians in west Germania. The Burgundian king was killed, tens of thousands of Burgundians slaughtered, and the great city of Augusta Vangionum burned. In the weeks of plunder that followed, thousands more were displaced, fleeing the region.

The battle took place many miles from Nanterre. Nonetheless, hordes of refugees flooded westward. Strange people sulked about the roads leading in and out of the village, speaking in foreign tongues and seeking a new home in the district. Rumors spread of Hunnic mercenaries from Asia pillaging and burning farmsteads outside Nanterre, while Burgundian refugees accosted caravans along the roads outside of France, killing merchants and seizing their goods. The Franks, too, took advantage of the chaos, continuing their plunder in the north. In addition to the violence, reports of disease and starvation spread far and wide. Flavius Aetius, meanwhile, returned to Ravenna to the court of Emperor Valentian, leaving Gaul to deal with the aftereffects of his victory.

In Nanterre, bands of refugees passed through. Though the townspeople provided them food and shelter for the night, they quickly sent the strangers away the following morning. Danger lurked all around them, sparking distrust. Genevieve, when she could, spoke to the refugees, asking them about their experiences and learning from them. From their stories, she got a sense of foreboding, of Nanterre being surrounded by a great noose on the verge of tightening.

On a brisk day in November, several Burgundian wanderers came into Nanterre, perhaps a dozen of them, clothed in rags and sores covering their skin, their eyes sunken with illness. They begged for bread at Saint Justin's. Mucianus and the women took pity on them, welcoming them in. They stayed in town for the afternoon, bartering for blankets and other supplies before moving off by sunset.

The following day, a farmer came running into town. "They're dead! They're all dead!"

"Who?" a woman asked. "Who has died?"

"The Burgundians! The travelers from yesterday!"

Whispers of a plague began to circulate through the village. Some fled, while others thought it was all an overreaction.

Several days later, their fears were confirmed. Mucianus fell ill, coughing violently and spitting up blood. Red sores appeared all over his flesh, and his body was drenched in sweat. He trembled under the covers, cold and hot all at once.

It was true: the Burgundians had brought the plague.

Life quickly broke down in Nanterre. Sickness cropped up everywhere. Some people dropped what they were doing and fled, others locked themselves in their homes. The priest Quintilian had gone missing the day after Mucianus took ill; whether he had fled or been killed on the road, nobody could say. In his absence and with Mucianus so sick, Genevieve became the default leader of the Church in Nanterre. She and her companions worked tirelessly as they ministered to the sick. They went door to door, leaving jugs of fresh water and bread outside the homes of those who had been afflicted. Mucianus soon died, but there was no time to grieve for him. The girls struggled to heave the old man's corpse out and delicately place him, with as much respect as they could, in a ditch behind the church where plague victims were being buried.

It was not long before illness entered Genevieve's own household. One of the other virgins began coughing, then another. Within a day, all four of the consecrated women save Genevieve were lying ill in the little house beside the church, wracked with violent coughing and covered in painful sores. Genevieve cared for each and prayed desperately for God to save them. Her prayers would go unanswered.

One by one, the girls died. Similar scenes were playing out in homes throughout Nanterre.

The First Sunday of Advent was a bitterly cold day. Genevieve, wrapped in a shawl and a pair of gloves she found in Mucianus's quarters, dragged the stiff bodies of her companions out of the house. A blistering wind swirled through the empty streets while Genevieve struggled, laboriously pulling one body after another across the churchyard to be deposited into the mass grave. After it was done, Genevieve knelt on the frozen earth, made the sign of the cross, and recited the traditional prayers for the dead.

As she rose, she realized she was not certain there was anyone left in town. Those who were strong enough had long since fled, those who had locked themselves indoors refused all communication with the outside. Was anyone still alive?

She walked up the street from the church. The town was eerily still, no sound save for the wind and the occasional banging of a door or shutter. Chickens and farm animals meandered, having been abandoned by their owners.

"Hello? Is anyone here?" Genevieve cried out.

The dark windows of the houses stared back at her, mute.

She decided to return to her parents' house. Though she had not seen them since the outbreak began, she had been praying for them daily. She knew they were isolated on their farmstead outside of town.

They should be safe. Papa is a smart man. He'd lock the doors and wait this out.

Despite what she told herself, her stomach felt queasy as she came up the road. Her family home looked the same as ever: the squat stone farmhouse with its thatched roof, barns, fieldstone fencing, and the dark Mont Valérien looming behind it. But something was off. It did not feel like her home but rather a twisted version of it from some nightmare. She broke into a run, hiking up her tunic as she darted up the gravel pathway. "Mama! Papa!" she called out into the wind. The windows were dark.

She approached the door, making the sign of the cross before opening it. "God help me," she said.

She pushed at the door. It creaked open.

The house was dark, still, cold. Her lip quivered.

If they were all right, there would be a fire burning.

"Mama? Papa?" she whispered.

No answer.

She walked inside, into the stillness. Layers of dust covered the floor, the furniture. She knelt and put her hand in the ashes of the fireplace. Cold.

Then she saw them. Lying together on their cot in the corner of the house. The blankets were pulled up over their heads, obscuring them. "Papa?" she called again. Tears welled in the corners of her eyes. Genevieve reached out with trembling hands and pulled down the covers. Her parents' lifeless gaze stared back at her, their sockets sunken and dry.

She turned away, clasping at her mouth. She fell to the floor, shaking. "Christ, help me, Christ, help me, Christ, help me," she mumbled over and over again.

She turned back, looking at her parents. Their skin had begun to shrivel and rot. They had been dead for some time, possibly a month or more. How could this have been? The plague only broke out three weeks ago when the Burgundian refugees came through town.

Then it hit her: the refugees had come from the east. If they walked to Nanterre on the eastern road, her parents' farmstead would have been the first house they encountered. They probably stopped here first, before they even came to the church. Severus and Gerontia, kind souls that they were, had probably helped them. It was likely that her parents were the first victims of the plague.

Tears streamed down her face while the sixteen-year-old girl lugged her parents' bodies from the house and stacked them in the cart her mother used to move alfalfa with. She choked on her tears while she grabbed an adze—a tool like a hoe—from the barn. Her sobbing mingled with the howling wind as she pushed the heavy cart up the hillside, to the line of trees that circled the base of Mont Valérien. The sheep—in their winter pens—rushed to Genevieve, baaing desperately. They were weak and emaciated; it must have been two weeks since anyone had fed them. "Go away! I've got nothing for you! There's nothing for you!" The sheep surrounded her, pressing in, nudging her with their noses and bleating for food. She struck them angrily. "Get out of here! Leave me alone!"

She pressed on until she came to the Green Circle, though it was green no more. Twisted brambles and the branches of naked trees clawed at each other in the wind. She picked up the adze and began chopping away the earth beneath her feet. She sobbed and convulsed, channeling all her energy into her work. The ground was hard but not yet frozen. When the trench was deep enough, she tilted the cart. Severus and Gerontia slid unceremoniously into the cold earth. She covered them hastily with dirt. Then taking the cart to the sheep enclosure, she used the adze to break a large pile of stones off the wall. These she brought back and piled upon the tomb as a sort of cairn. She did this not only to mark the spot but as a practical matter to keep scavenging animals from digging up the shallow grave. This being done, she tied two sticks together into a rough cross and thrust it into the cairn.

By the time they were buried, night had fallen. Her hands were raw from working the adze, and her arms ached from dragging bodies all day. She wiped her nose on her sleeve the way children do, then sniffling, dried her eyes. "Requiéscant in pace," she said weakly, making the sign of the cross. "Farewell, Papa and Mama. I'll pray for you. And you, pray for your daughter."

Genevieve stumbled out of the Green Circle. The sheep gathered near the enclosure wall where she had pried the stones loose. They had learned to keep their distance from the girl, and they did not like the look of the adze in her hand, but they still stared with looks of pathetic desperation.

Genevieve was no longer angry; she felt bad for them. She went to the wall and continued to break it down with the adze, ripping the stones out one at a time. Finally, she had created an opening large enough for the sheep to pass through. They gawked at the opening, unsure what to make of it.

"Go!" Genevieve commanded. "You're free!" She raised the adze in the air and whistled as her father used to do when it was time to move the herd. They flowed through the opening, out into the fields. "Go! You're on your own!" she called. "We're all on our own!"

The sheep wandered aimlessly until they found their way to Severus's barn, where the alfalfa was kept. Once this was discovered, the sheep had a feast that would have been sang of for generations—if sheep could sing.

Genevieve turned and walked into the night, dragging the adze upon the earth behind her.

Chapter 6

The Enemy Rears Its Head

Genevieve could not bring herself to stay at home or in the room attached to the church where her friends had recently perished. Instead, she stayed in the sanctuary of Saint Justin's, sleeping on a cot in the corner and pouring her tears out before the altar day after day. Slowly, those who had fled Nanterre trickled back into town, and people who had been holed up inside their homes cautiously ventured out. But there were too few left for life to return to normal, too many dead. The village was a shell of its former self. And with everyone she knew dead, there really was no returning to normal for Genevieve either.

A few days before Christmas, the girl packed some personal items in a sack, donned an extra woolen tunic, and set off on foot for Paris. Upon her arrival, Bishop Vivianus received her compassionately. The good bishop was aware of the devastation unfolding across the countryside and agreed to let Genevieve live with some of the widows of the Christian community of Paris, women who were too old to remarry and so lived a semi-monastic existence in a large old villa not far from Saint Etienne's. She celebrated Christmas in the cathedral, offering tearful prayers for the repose of the souls of her loved ones.

Work kept Genevieve busy as the women assigned her to do the laundering and cooking for the little community. She was appreciative of the work but still felt desolate inside. She wondered if she would ever feel joy again. In Nanterre, she had been popular and outgoing. Here in Paris among the widows, she was shy, withdrawn, sullen. The women called her "the quiet one." Though Genevieve was surrounded by people, she had no friends.

In her heartache, she turned to Christ, spending every spare moment in the candlelit repose of Saint Etienne's, sometimes as still as a statue, sometimes weeping bitterly, but always offering her heart to God. She remembered how Patricius had said he prayed one hundred times a day and one hundred times a night in Ireland. When she was younger, she would retreat to the Green Circle and count her prayers, happy if she got to twenty. She smiled. Now her prayers seemed less quantifiable. When she went into the church, she was not sure how many times she prayed. It seemed now like one unending circle of prayer.

She also began fasting, generally taking meals of beans and bread only a few times per week. Her face grew austere, and she walked about with her head downcast, often praying to herself. The women of the community began grumbling about her.

"Look at the little hypocrite," they would say. "She thinks she's a saint!"

Some even mocked her sorrow.

"Does she think she's the only one who has suffered tragedy? The little brat! We've all suffered. What makes her special?"

These calumnies were too much for Genevieve. She went to Vivianus, and throwing herself at the bishop's feet, begged his aid.

"You've struggled these past few months," said Vivianus. "Perhaps I have erred by keeping you secluded with the widows. I think some works of mercy would be good for your soul, and it will get you out of the city awhile."

"Oh, yes, please!" Genevieve pleaded, clutching the hem of Vivianus's tunic. "That would be a blessing to my soul. Whatever you command, I will do it."

"Well, now, hold on," the bishop said, "it's dangerous out there. There's more chaos in the world every day. Who knows what you'd encounter on the open road? Franks. Huns. Burgundians. Thieves."

"Please, sir, I'd rather take my chances with a Frank than be cooped up in this house with these bitter women one more day."

Vivianus smiled. "I see you are still hasty and crave adventure. Very well! May God reward you."

From then on, Genevieve was entrusted with visiting the villages and homesteads around Paris on errands of mercy, not unlike what Patricius had once done in Nanterre—delivering food to the poor of the countryside, tending to the sick, bringing clothes and offerings from the Christians of Paris to distribute, delivering letters from the bishop to his presbyters. Vivianus usually arranged things so that Genevieve did not have to travel alone but instead was accompanied by merchants or acolytes from the Church. But when she did receive time alone on the roads, she treasured the solitude. The countryside around Paris was filled with rolling fields and crisscrossed by numberless little brooks that fed into the Seine. As winter turned to spring and spring to summer, the pleasant air returned and warmed Genevieve's heart. She still ached for her family and friends every day, but she again began to delight in the brightness of the sun and the green of the trees and the laughter of the water splashing down the pebble-strewn rivulets on its way to the Seine.

One summer day, Genevieve stopped off at a cluster of cottages to call on the families there. It was a lovely little spot, a gently sloping hill planted with crops. Ducks and swine rummaged about, and dirty children ran barefoot, chasing each other with sticks. A poor existence but happy. Genevieve smiled as she watched the children play their simple game, watched over by their mothers, their fathers out in the fields.

As Genevieve stopped to hand over a few blankets and speak with the women, one of the children ran up to hand her a flower. "Why, thank you!" said Genevieve. The boy said nothing, looking up at her with a beaming smile. "You're very kind," she added, putting her hand on the side of the boy's face. The boy's eyes grew wide, and his mouth dropped open. He began to scream, turning to run into a nearby cottage.

Everyone rushed after the boy except Genevieve, who was left standing alone with the flower. Inside the cottage, she could hear a babble of voices, crying, shouting, laughing.

What on earth did I do?

When the boy's mother ran out of the cottage, Genevieve cried, "I'm sorry! I don't know what I did. I didn't mean to harm the boy!"

"Harmed? Lord, no! You've worked a miracle!"

"Excuse me?"

"Carlo has been deaf since birth. But at your touch, he received his hearing."

"What?"

"He's never heard sound before. The noises of the world startled him."

Everyone flooded out of the cottage. They looked at Genevieve with a mix of fear and awe. "Praise Christ and the saints!" they called. They surrounded her, bowing their heads and clutching at her tunic as if it were a holy relic.

"No," Genevieve protested, "please, there has been a mistake."

Carlo stepped out of the cottage, his face shining. The other children circled around him. "Carlo, can you hear this? Can you hear my voice?"

Carlo laughed and nodded.

"You're a saint!" one woman cried to Genevieve.

Genevieve forced a smile. "God bless you," she whispered. She handed the flower to Carlo's mother and turned to run, coming before Vivianus hours later. She hoped the bishop would have some advice or understanding about the matter, but all he did was make the sign of the cross. "Praise God, my child. Let us praise God for this miracle."

News of what happened spread throughout the countryside. The people praised Genevieve as a wonderworker, but her fame only embittered her detractors, including a certain presbyter named Desiderius, who was convinced that Genevieve was a fraud. He fed into the widows' resentment of Genevieve so much that they pushed their way into her cell one day, forcibly dragged her out, and threw her into the street, calling her names and beating her with sticks.

Vivianus was mortified. He could not believe that these women he had handed Genevieve over to, these Christian widows, let alone one of his own presbyters, would be involved in such wickedness. He summoned Desiderius to answer for his actions, forbidding him from ministering in Paris or having any further contact with the widows.

"As for Genevieve," the bishop thundered, "she is under my personal protection. You will harass her no more, or I will exile you from this city."

Desiderius sulked away, cowed into submission but fuming with resentment. As for Genevieve, Vivianus gave her a private cell in the complex of Saint Etienne's. "Stay here until this situation settles down," the bishop told her.

Her new cell was sparse, but at least she had peace. Genevieve occupied her time praying, cleaning Saint Etienne's, and doing menial tasks like washing the altar linens and making candles. As she worked, she kept thinking about that day at the cottage, about why God had chosen to work a miracle through her. She did not feel worthy. She did not feel like a saint.

One day toward the end of the summer, Genevieve walked down to the Seine to draw water for laundering. It was a bright day in early August, hot and humid. The sky was deep blue, and boats floated along the river. The mood of the day brought back the memory of when she made her vows in the presence of her mother. The memory was bittersweet, both wonderful and heartbreaking all at once. So much had changed since that day.

The place where she drew water from was obscured by bushes and overshadowed by a venerable old willow tree. Genevieve knelt by the bank and set her jugs beside the tree. Slipping her shoes off, she dipped her feet in the cool water. Genevieve removed her veil, folded it carefully, and set it down. She scooped a handful of water and splashed it on her head, running her fingers through her short, blond hair. Her braids fell forward, resting upon her collarbone.

Then suddenly, someone was on her, rough hands gripping her neck and thrusting her down toward the water! Genevieve resisted but had not the strength to match her attacker. Just before her head plunged into the river, she heard a raspy voice shout, "Shove her head down!" She held her breath until she was able to lift her head back above the water—only for a moment—until she was thrust back under. Water flushed through her nose. She kicked and thrashed.

Jesus, help me! Someone is trying to drown me!

Then just as suddenly as the attack had begun, the hands released her. Genevieve emerged from the water, coughing, crying, spitting up water. Two men she did not know were being pulled from the river by Vivianus and his deacons.

There was a great deal of shouting and struggling, but she was too overwhelmed to comprehend it.

"Genevieve," a soft voice broke her trance. "Come, come out of the water." She looked up. One of the deacons had his hand extended toward her. She grasped it and allowed him to shepherd her out of the river.

An hour later, Genevieve sat crying on her bed, her cold body shivering from her damp clothes. "Dear God," she cried over and over again. "What happened? Why?"

A knock rattled at the door, and the bishop entered with a swarm of attendants. Genevieve was given a blanket to wrap up in, and a deacon handed her the veil she'd left folded by the tree. Genevieve kissed it, put it back atop her wet, matted hair, and tucked her braids into it. The bishop took a chair, flanked by his hosts who stood about him like courtiers around a king.

"Genevieve, how are you feel—"

"—why on earth would they want to drown me?" Genevieve shouted. "I've never seen those men in my life!"

"We're still looking into it. But we believe they were paid by Desiderius."

"Desiderius the presbyter? A priest of the Church paid to have me drowned?"

"It would seem so," said Vivianus, sighing. "I'm terribly sorry, my dear."

"What have I done to him to arouse such enmity?"

"The fault is partially mine," said Vivianus. "I've been keeping things from you."

"What do you mean?"

He sighed again. "Earlier this year, you worked a miracle in the countryside, healing the deaf boy."

"I didn't mean to," Genevieve protested.

"Never mind about that," Vivianus said dismissively. "The fact is there's been other miracles, too."

"Other miracles?"

"Indeed. Several of the people you've visited and prayed for have been healed. The reports have been coming in all summer."

"Surely, you are mistaken!"

"I am certainly not," said the bishop, motioning to an attendant. The young man stepped forward and handed Vivianus a scroll. The bishop unrolled and began to read. "Lucianus, age forty-two, farmer, healed of gout. Mariella, age fifty-nine, widow, healed of blindness. Wolfric, age thirty-six, a laborer, asked your prayers about his situation in April."

"I remember! He is deeply in debt with no means of paying it off."

"Not anymore," said Vivianus plainly. "A week after your visit, he was digging in his garden, and he found a golden goblet. He sold it in Paris for a year's wages."

Genevieve's jaw dropped. "That can't be!"

"Oh, yes, and there are many more. You are a wonder-worker, Genevieve. We must praise God for you!"

The bishop and all the attendants crossed themselves.

"How could you have kept these things from me?" Genevieve asked.

"That was my error," said Vivianus. "The one miracle you were aware of, and the troubles with the widows, it all seemed so hard on you. I wanted to let you spend the summer here in peace, without worry. But then these stories started coming in. Everyone was talking about you. Desiderius was given over to envy, and because he had persecuted you, the Church here held him in disdain. A month ago, he abandoned the diocese altogether, and I have not seen him since. He's been corrupted by the evil one. From what these men tell me, Desiderius paid them a handsome sum to kill you. They've been lurking about Saint Etienne's the past few days, waiting for their chance."

Genevieve was silent.

"I should have trusted God," the bishop continued. "He is working through you, Genevieve."

"And what of the men?" she said sternly. "What is their punishment to be?"

One of the attendants, a clerk, said, "Laying hands on a consecrated woman? Lying in wait and attempted murder? They must be put to death."

"I see," she said. "May I speak with them?"

"I hardly think that's appropriate," said Vivianus.

"I'd like to see them," Genevieve repeated. "Please don't deny me this."

Vivianus thought for a moment, then relented. "As you wish. You may see them in the sanctuary in an hour."

After the men left, Genevieve quickly changed, brushed her hair, and made herself presentable. She came down into the church with time to spare, praying before the Lord for some time before the heavy doors creaked open and the men were brought in. Genevieve stood and turned, facing her attackers. Their hands were bound by cords, and each was guarded by several officials and clergy. They no longer looked as frightening as they did by the river. Their heads were downcast, their bodies trembling. Genevieve felt flashes of panic coming before them again, but she also pitied them. They looked pathetic and were obviously of very poor means.

"Here are the men," said Vivianus. "They will be taken to the magistrate after your interview."

Genevieve stood tall, looking directly at them. "Why did you want to drown me?"

The men waited for the other to answer. Finally, one man cleared his throat. "We got nothing against you, ma'am. Was the priest Desiderius who put us up to it."

"Aye," said the other. "He said if we'n take care o' this problem for him, he'd pay us fine, six solidi *each*! An' me and Rusticus here, that's six-month worth a coin for both o' us!"

"We ne'er killed any folk before," said Rusticus. "But the priest was awful angry with you, ma'am. Said we'd be doing the Church a favor if we took you off. Ain't that right, Corus?"

Corus nodded quickly. "An' he said we'd get an extra solidus if we made it look like an accident! So, Rusticus and I were fixin' to make it look like you was drowned."

"Enough of this, you oafs!" the bishop boomed. "Where is Desiderius now?"

"We don't know, sir," said Rusticus. "We was supposed to find him at the gate after the deed was done, but I expect he ain't gonna show, now he heard we've been caught."

"They're going to execute you both, do you realize that?" said Genevieve. "You'll be dead by this time next week."

"Oh, no, please!" they cried. Both dropped to their knees in supplication. "Ma'am, honest, we got nothing against you! We woulda never thought of it if that priest hadn't put us up to it! He was the one who came seeking us out! Don't kill us! Let us be your slaves! Anything!"

"Listen to this blathering!" said one of the officials. "They're going to make a fine spectacle when they swing from the noose."

At the mention of a noose, the men broke down into tears.

"Quiet!" barked Genevieve. The men clammed up, surprised at the power in the girl's voice. Turning to the bishop, she said, "Vivianus, I think it's clear Rusticus and Corus are mere stooges. Desiderius is the real villain. Release these men at once. I forgive them."

The men's eyes widened. Vivianus looked flustered. "Genevieve," he said "these men are scoundrels. They're—"

"—they are under *my* judgment, and their lives are forfeited to *me*," Genevieve interjected forcefully. "And I say I forgive them. Let them go."

Vivianus looked at the city officials.

"If the lady doesn't want charges," one said, "she is within her rights to request their release."

Vivianus sighed. "Release them."

After the men's cords were cut, they fell on their faces, clutching the hem of Genevieve's tunic. "Forgive us, lady! Pray for us sinners! We are in your debt!"

"Go in peace," said Genevieve gently. "But remember, God has given you your lives back this day. Do not provoke him again. You will not receive a second chance."

They thanked her again before scampering out of Saint Etienne's.

"Those two will be at it again in no time," the clerk murmured.

"On my honor, sir, I vouch that they will not," Genevieve snapped. The clerk bowed in deference, saying nothing further.

Genevieve turned to the bishop, "My good Vivianus, I know you mean well, and you have been a dear father to me since I've been here. But please, I beg you, hide no more from me."

Vivianus nodded, "I won't, my dear Genevieve. You have my word."

The bishop was not the only one moved by Genevieve's act of clemency. Her mercy became the gossip of Paris. People came from all around to see her, speak with her, or receive her blessing. Even the Parisian widows reconciled with her, apologizing for their cruelty and welcoming her back into their villa. And from the day Genevieve returned, they lived in perfect harmony.

As for Desiderius, nobody could say what had become of him.

Chapter 7

Saint Genevieve of Paris

Genevieve settled into life in Paris. Though there were no more reports of miracles for the time being, people from all around came to seek her prayers. The commotion about Genevieve was so great that Bishop Vivianus decided it was no longer prudent to house her with the widows, who preferred things a little quieter. He moved Genevieve to new quarters attached to the episcopal residence. But she was not alone there. Ever since her arrival, other young girls had come to Paris, seeking to enter religious life. Genevieve was put in charge of the formation of these young women.

While it was good to once again live among girls her own age, Genevieve's obligations left her feeling overwhelmed. When she could find time, she prostrated herself before the Lord in the cathedral. Head pressed to the stone floor, she said, "Lord, I am only a young woman, and you've made me a mother over these girls! I'm still a child myself. I don't know how to lead. Show me the way!" She poured her heart out in this way for many days.

Her prayers were answered by the arrival of a very distinguished visitor. Tales of Genevieve's miracles had reached Auxerre, and when Germanus heard that the little girl he had met on the road years ago was now leading a religious community, he set off to visit her in Paris.

Genevieve waited for him on the road outside the gates of the city, as she used to watch the little road that went through Nanterre. The good bishop spied her some distance off, his face beaming through his white beard. When he approached, he called from his horse, "Lo, girl, I appear to be lost. Can you tell me the way to Paris?"

"Father Germanus!" Genevieve laughed. "What a joy it is to meet you on the road again!" She took the bishop's hand and kissed it. "May I guide you into the city?"

"By all means."

She took his horse by the reins and walked before the bishop, leading him through the gates of Paris. Townsfolk had gathered to watch, wanting to catch a glimpse of the holy man. "A saint leading a saint!" the Parisians said as they watched Genevieve lead the venerable man through the streets of the city.

After Germanus paid a customary visit to Bishop Vivianus and greeted the Parisian clergy, he spent time talking with Genevieve in the gardens outside the cathedral. Genevieve's novices brought stools, and the two sat beside the Seine, watching the women weed the cabbage patch while they talked.

"They seem disciplined," observed Germanus. "How many girls have been put in your charge?"

"Twenty," sighed Genevieve, "and more arrive each week."

Germanus nodded. "Impressive. In Auxerre, our convent has thirty, and it was established decades ago. I believe you will outpace us by year's end."

"Oh, Germanus, it's not a contest!" Genevieve laughed.

He smiled. "Well, why do you think they are all coming?"

"What do you mean?"

"It's because of *you*, Genevieve. They are here because of you. You've inspired them."

Genevieve put her head into her hands. "Germanus, that can't be. I don't know what I'm doing!"

The old man chuckled. "Do you think Moses knew what he was doing when he wandered up onto Mount Horeb and found the burning bush? Or Peter when Our Lord told him to step out of the boat?" He leaned in, striking his breast, and whispered, "Do you think *I* knew what I was doing when I founded the Abbey of Auxerre? Or Patricius the night he fled slavery in Ireland? That's not how faith works, my dear."

"I know, I know, but—"

The old man held up his hand and shushed her. "Listen," he said, "how do you learn to walk?"

"By . . . walking?" Genevieve said.

"Exactly. You learn to walk by walking, to believe by believing. And you learn to govern by governing. So, have faith, govern your girls, and God will bless you."

"But what if I make mistakes?" Genevieve protested. "Souls are in my hand. What if I fail? I'm so clumsy and impetuous."

"God factored that in when he called you to this," Germanus said.

Genevieve took a breath and looked out at her young novices on their hands and knees amidst the cabbage rows, tunics mired in dirt, working the earth with their hands. "I suppose what you say is comforting. This is all God's work after all."

"It is indeed. We may plant and water, but God gives the bounty," Germanus said, pointing his finger heavenward.

"Poor Bishop Vivianus," Genevieve chuckled. "I don't think he knows what to do with me."

At the mention of Vivianus, Germanus's face went blank. A gray glaze fell over his eyes. "Vivianus will have no say in the matter soon enough," he said cryptically.

"Whatever do you mean by that?"

Germanus smiled weakly, but it looked forced. "Things are about to change for you."

"How? What . . . what will change? What does Vivianus have to do with this?"

"I'm sorry, my dear," Germanus mumbled. "I'm not feeling well. Please excuse me."

He rose quickly. Genevieve hesitated, then knelt before the old man and received his blessing.

"Christ grace you with abundant fruit in the Spirit," he placed his trembling hand upon her head. "God be with you, beloved daughter."

He retired to his quarters, leaving Genevieve to ponder his words. The next day, Germanus was gone.

A few weeks later, Bishop Vivianus suddenly fell ill and died. The clergy of the city gathered and elected a presbyter named

Flavian to succeed him. Flavian had been an ardent supporter of Genevieve during the time of Desiderius's persecution. Genevieve rejoiced at his appointment.

"Perhaps this is the change Germanus mentioned?" Genevieve mused.

Flavian's appointment was only the beginning of a cascade of changes. Soon after, word reached Paris that the dreaded Huns were spreading out over the entire country, raiding and pillaging. Their fearsome king, Attila, had already subjugated many peoples and was bent on adding Gaul to his Hunnic empire. Scouts of Duke Victorinus confirmed that not only was Attila heading west, but he intended to attack the city of Paris. The city was protected by only a small garrison, most of the troops being on campaign with Aetius, Victorinus, and the other lords. "We're going to be slaughtered!" people cried in the streets. Shops closed and people hid their valuables. People began slipping out of the city, hoping to find refuge further west. Soon the most eminent citizens of Paris were discussing abandoning the city entirely.

People clamored about outside the church, insisting that Flavian, Genevieve, and the clergy abandon the city as well. "To stay here is certain death!" they said.

Bishop Flavian met the crowd on the steps of the cathedral. "The Church of Paris was entrusted to me to shepherd. Shall I flee at the approach of the wolves? Such is not the way of a shepherd!"

Genevieve, too, resisted the calls to flee. "Where will you go?" she asked the crowd. "Where will you escape to?"

"We will flee west," a man cried. "Follow the Seine."

"Where?" Genevieve demanded. "Into the arms of the Franks? A horde of unarmed refugees pressing into the wilderness? They'll fall upon you and slaughter you within a week. Even if you made it through Frankish lands, then what? Britannia is falling, there's no security there. Wherever you go, you'll be exposed."

"I'd rather take my chances in the wilderness than wait here for Attila to butcher me!" a man yelled.

"Did you hear what he did at Vesontio?" a woman called. "He brought the entire town out onto the plains and slit their throats—women and children, too!"

The crowd degenerated into a hysterical chaos.

"We must leave!" the people said, turning from the church.

"Please, don't!" Genevieve pleaded. "Whatever awaits us, you'll be safer here behind the walls of Paris than out in the wilderness!"

Her warnings went unheeded. By the next day, it appeared that most Parisians were resolved to flee the city. People were loading wagons with food and supplies to prepare for flight. Seeing her words useless, Genevieve and the young women in her care resorted to prayer. After attending Mass and receiving Holy Communion from the hands of Bishop Flavian, they knelt and prayed before the altar of the cathedral. Tears flowed down Genevieve's face. She remembered the corpses of Nanterre. "Not again, Lord!" she sobbed. "Please, be with us!"

That day, a cloaked stranger rode swiftly toward Paris. The city gates were shut, but the stranger presented a letter to the guards. They admitted him immediately. The stranger spurred his horse on through the twisted, muddy streets of

Paris, dashing between the mobs of panicked citizens thronging the streets. He crossed the bridge over the Seine, pressing toward the Cathedral of Saint Etienne.

Bishop Flavian was gathered in the cathedral with the entire Parisian clergy, along with Genevieve and the consecrated women of the city, discussing the situation. The bishop's resolve was beginning to fade. "Perhaps the people are right," he said, downcast. "I wanted to stay with my flock. But if the flock itself abandons Paris, what good can we do here?"

At that moment, the doors of the cathedral burst open. Genevieve and the others turned. The rider, standing in the light, drew back his hood, revealing the square face of a battle-hardened man, scarred and worn from years of trial.

"Who are you?" asked Flavian. "What is your business here?"

The man strode up to the bishop. "I am Caelistinus, the archdeacon of Bishop Germanus of Auxerre. He has sent me here on an urgent errand."

Flavian raised his eyebrows. "You come from Germanus?"

Caelistinus turned his eyes to the women, eventually settling his gaze upon Genevieve. "Are you the virgin Genevieve?" he asked.

She nodded.

He pulled a bag from his cloak and placed it in Genevieve's hands. "This should establish the truth of what I say." Caelistinus stretched forth his arms, revealing dark tattoos. "Open it . . . *carefully*," he added.

Genevieve cautiously opened the sack. Inside, a letter and another smaller sack. She removed the letter and glanced over the scroll. "It's from Germanus!"

"What does he say?" asked Flavian.

"To Genevieve, my daughter in Christ, and to Flavian, Bishop of Paris, I say to you, stand fast. As a sign of our affection and prayers, receive the enclosed gift." Genevieve looked up. "That's all."

The bishop took the smaller sack from her and opened it. Upon seeing its contents, he made the sign of the cross. "Eulogies!" he exclaimed. The clergy all bowed their heads and likewise crossed themselves. The bishop removed the contents, three thin circles of unleavened bread like the kind used for the Eucharist.

"What are Eulogies?" asked Genevieve.

"Unconsecrated bread," replied Caelistinus. "Taken from the altar of Auxerre before the prayers of the liturgy."

"Yes," said Flavian, "Eulogies are gifts of unconsecrated bread bishops may send on special occasions as demonstrations of love and solidarity. It is a tangible sign of the prayers of the Church of Auxerre for us." Then turning to Caelistinus, Flavian bowed. "Thank you, Brother Caelistinus, for this gift. We will use this bread when we celebrate the Sacred Mysteries this very evening. Receiving Eulogies from the altar of the eminent Germanus in such a dire time is a great honor indeed."

Caelistinus smiled. "Do not forget, the honor is *hers*." He pointed to Genevieve. "Germanus sent them to Genevieve. In doing so, he counsels you to heed her." Having said this, the deacon donned his hood and turned to leave.

"Wait!" called Flavian, taking Caelistinus by the cloak. "Brother, forgive my hesitancy. But . . . well, you do not look the part of a deacon. And your mannerisms, they are almost militaristic."

"I did twenty years in the Roman legions," Caelistinus replied. "*Legio XXX, Ulpia Victrix*," he added, striking his breast. "After my enlistment, I joined the clergy. I suppose you can leave the army, but the army never quite leaves you."

"Oh, Caelistinus, please stay!" Genevieve pleaded, kneeling and taking the deacon's cloak. "We could use your counsel."

"Yes, Brother," added the bishop. "Your advice would be most welcome."

"Germanus puts great confidence in this young woman," Caelistinus said. "It's your advice we should heed. What do you think should be done?"

Genevieve thought a moment, then said, "Caelistinus, when you were in the military, how did the soldiers defend their encampment?"

"We would guard the camp on a watch," he said. "Men would take shifts on a rotation, so the camp was always protected."

"Exactly," said Genevieve. "I suggest we adopt this method for the spiritual defense of Paris."

"How so?" asked Flavian.

"We organize a prayer watch. Let the Christians of Paris come here and intercede with the Lord for our deliverance. The faithful can be divided into rotations and take different shifts, so there is always someone here before the altar, pleading our cause."

"Yes," said Caelistinus. "And in this way, we can fulfill Saint Paul's admonition to pray without ceasing! Bishop Flavian, what do you say?"

The bishop folded his hands humbly. "Who can deny the providence of Brother Caelistinus coming to us in our darkest moment to strengthen our hearts? Let us do as Genevieve suggests. Perhaps God will heed our prayers, but if we, too, die, we will die here at our post like Christians and Romans."

When word got out that Germanus had sent Eulogies to Genevieve, many citizens reconsidered their plans and resolved to stay. "Germanus is a very saintly bishop," they said to one another. "The Eulogies are a sign from God that we should stay, as Genevieve says."

Genevieve and Caelistinus worked relentlessly over the following days to recruit adorers for their prayer rotation. People started trickling into the cathedral in shifts. They were organized by Genevieve's sisters and led in their devotions by Flavian and his clergy. The adoration was slow at first, but within a few days, the cathedral was packed round the clock with Parisians praying for deliverance. The Mass where Flavian consecrated the Eulogies of Germanus saw the cathedral fuller than anyone could remember. In the end, only a handful of Parisians ended up fleeing the city.

That very afternoon, word came that an army approached Paris from the east. The people grew worried but remained calm, steeling their hearts in prayer. The gates were locked, the walls manned, and every household secured their goods. The prayers continued solemnly in the cathedral. Whatever would be would be.

Then suddenly, fear gave way to elation. The army was not Hunnic but Roman. The Parisians surged to the walls of the city to behold the site. "Could it be true?" Genevieve said to her religious sisters. "Have we truly been delivered?"

The scene at the city gates was chaotic as thousands of Parisians milled about, trying to peer out.

"Make way for Genevieve the Virgin!" someone called. At her name, the crowd parted like the Red Sea. Genevieve passed through, leading a dozen sisters.

"It's her prayers that saved us!" a woman whispered.

"We have our own saint—Saint Genevieve of Paris!" another said.

"Saint Genevieve of Paris!" people began to call out. The crowd erupted in applause.

Genevieve smiled and waved weakly, keeping her eyes downcast. *Pride goeth before a fall*, she prayed silently.

The captain of the gates looked down from his watch station. "Lady Genevieve!" he called. "Come up here and look! See our deliverance!" Genevieve was hustled to the gates and helped up the ladder to the watch station, a platform behind the great wooden palisade that formed the main defense of the city. "Up you go," said the captain, pulling Genevieve up by the arm.

From the height of the watch station, Genevieve had a clear view of the countryside for some miles around. Massing on the fields outside the city, one could see a vast army of mounted warriors bearing the standards of Rome. The sea of riders swept out over the plains as far as Genevieve could see.

"I've never seen an army so large," she marveled.

"It is the *magister militum*, Lord Aetius himself," said the captain with pride. "The highest authority in the Roman army."

"God certainly heard our prayers," Genevieve whispered, crossing herself.

"It seems God doesn't answer your prayers by half-measures," the captain laughed.

"Sir!" called a guard. "A detachment from the army is approaching the city!"

Indeed, a handful of riders had broken from the main force and were galloping toward the gates.

"The imperial standard. That is Aetius himself!" exclaimed the captain. "Open the gates!"

Soldiers hustled to the heavy wooden gates, cranking the lever. The gates lurched open. Three riders headed the entourage. Bearing the imperial standard was Duke Victorinus, wrapped in his cloak of gray, though considerably older than the last time Genevieve saw him, now wearing a stubbly gray beard to match. At the head was an older man garbed in a golden tunic rimmed with white and a bright blue cloak with an elaborate golden clasp. His face was grim and solemn, the face of a man who had borne more than his share of responsibilities and stresses.

"That is Aetius, the *magister militum*," said the captain.

"Who is the third rider?" Genevieve pointed. "The boy in the rough-hewn tunic?"

"That would be Childeric, young Prince of the Franks."

"The Franks are fighting on our side?"

"At least the Salian tribe," answered the captain. "Childeric and his father, Merovech, have allied with Aetius. The

Franks and Romans, we may have our differences, but the Franks don't want to be part of Attila's Hunnic empire any more than we do. It's an alliance of convenience."

"He's so young!" she said. "He can't be older than fourteen. When I was his age, I was focused on sheep. I can't imagine the horrors he has seen at such a young age!"

The grateful Parisians cheered as the entourage entered the gates, some flinging themselves on their knees in thanksgiving, exclaiming, *"Vīvat Roma!"* and "God bless Aetius!"

"People of Paris," called Aetius in a thick, raspy voice, "I bring you tidings of good news. The army of Attila has moved off to the south. We think he is going to attack Orléans. My army—aided by the Franks and other federated tribes—are heading there to intercept him."

"Paris is safe?" someone cried.

"Nothing is safe in these dark times," said Aetius solemnly. "But for now, the threat of Attila has moved off."

Genevieve sighed and collapsed against the palisade. The anxiety and work of the last week had made her forget how exhausted she was. Aetius's words lifted a burden she scarcely knew she was carrying. She trembled.

"Are you all right, Genevieve?" asked the captain, steadying the young woman with his arm.

Victorinus glanced up at the watch station. When he saw Genevieve, he raised his gloved hand, a small smile brightening his hardened face, at least for a moment. Regaining her composure, Genevieve saluted the duke, her polished bronze ring gleaming in the sun. At the sight of the shining ring, a tear welled up in the corner of his eyes and rolled, uninhibited, down his stubbled face. When the Frankish Prince

Childeric caught sight of the Roman's tears, he turned his gaze up to Genevieve. For a moment, their gaze locked, and he blinked darkly at her.

Two weeks later, the army of Aetius fought Attila's Huns outside Orléans. It was a vast battle that saw thousands killed on both sides. The Roman army barely held out, but at the end of the day, Attila was forced to retreat from Gaul, never to return.

Aetius celebrated a hard-earned victory, but the news was bitter, for Duke Victorinus had fallen. The duke's body, laden with many wounds, was sent to Paris, where Genevieve and her sisters lovingly prepared him for his burial. Caelistinus, the old military man, presided over the funeral rites. Genevieve watched Victorinus's body as it was lowered into the damp earth, where it would rest until the Lord called forth the dead at the consummation of the world.

Chapter 8

No Earthly Eden

Genevieve rubbed her fingers together as she blew on them. The December wind swirled off the plains, whipping her ankle-length tunic against her legs. A train of people, far as the eye could see, stretched out before her, winding their way up the road to the Paris gates.

"They look so miserable!" lamented Sister Floriana.

"They *are* miserable," Genevieve said. "So many have had to leave their homes to seek refuge inside the walls of Paris. The world is in chaos."

"I cannot believe this is happening again," said Floriana. "How many flooded into our city this spring?"

"Things are getting worse," Genevieve said. "The Frankish raids are pushing deeper into our lands. The countryside is not safe anymore."

"Mother, how are we going to care for so many refugees?" asked Floriana.

Genevieve sighed. "That is a good question.

The refugees, drawn from the villages surrounding Paris, were dirty and shabbily clothed. Their sunken faces, their emaciated bodies, spoke of their desperation. Many drove animals before them: sheep, goats, swine. A flock of sheep bleated at Genevieve as their keeper drove them by.

"You know, I was once a shepherdess," Genevieve mused.

"No. You? Really?"

"It's true," she said. "Long ago, I was a barefoot country girl. I scarcely knew the world outside my family's pasture."

"It is fitting," Floriana said. "You have a shepherd's heart. That is why you're the pillar of the Church here in Paris."

Genevieve scoffed. "Don't say such foolishness! You know the bishop is the pillar of the Church."

Floriana shrugged. "You are a more permanent fixture in Paris than the bishop. In the decade since Flavian died, we've gone through four bishops. Before Pallus arrived, we were without one for eight months. Nobody wants to come here. It's no wonder people look to you for hope."

"It's the chaos of the times," said Genevieve coldly. "But enough of this prattle; we were supposed to count the refugees. How many do you think we've seen?"

"It's scarcely midmorning, and I'd say we've seen a thousand already."

"And they will continue to come all day," said Genevieve. "I suppose there's no need for us to linger here. Let us go tell Bishop Pallus what we've seen."

The two women wrapped their tunics around them as they turned back toward the city.

"Saint Genevieve!" someone cried.

Genevieve turned back. A middle-aged woman with two young children—one on each hip—clambered toward her. Her hair was ragged, her face smeared with grime. "Saint Genevieve!" she called again. "Bless my children and I!" The woman dropped to her knees before Genevieve and bowed her head.

Genevieve gently lifted the woman to her feet. "I am honored, but I am no saint, just a Christian woman trying to make the best of things. Nor am I a priest, so I cannot give you a priestly blessing, but tell me your name, and I will pray for you."

"Anna," she answered. "Yes, please, remember me in your prayers. My husband, he was killed by the Franks. They burned our farm. We have nothing."

The woman began to sob.

Sister Floriana stepped forward. "Anna, let me carry those children for you. Come, I'll take you into the city." Anna, still sobbing, handed the grubby children to Floriana. "I'll see you at prayers, Mother," Floriana said.

Genevieve nodded, forcing a weak smile. "I'll remember your family, Anna. The Lord be gracious to you!"

Genevieve made her way back into Paris, drifting with the tide of refugees flooding through the gates. Her mind flitted over the events of the past decade and all the turmoil Gaul had faced. The victory over Attila saved Paris from destruction just to pave the way for a slow death. Aetius's success had only aroused the envy of Emperor Valentinian, who had him executed soon after. Then Valentinian himself was assassinated. Since then, the imperial throne bounced between the favorites of barbarian warlords, the true powers behind the throne. The countryside, meanwhile, was overrun by Franks, Visigoths, Burgundians, and scores of other lesser tribes. The Roman people, at the mercy of the barbarian marauders, could expect no relief from Rome.

Paris, too, had suffered immensely. Duke Victorinus was never replaced, leaving the city to the governance of its bishops. But they, too, came and went with dizzying frequency. The new bishop, Pallus, was a meek man, good hearted but too timid to take on the challenges facing him. The city was descending into anarchy, pulled apart by rival factions.

Genevieve thought of her departed friend.

What I wouldn't give to talk to Germanus. Every human pillar I've ever relied on has been taken away. All I have is God.

Making the sign of the cross, she mouthed the words of the seventeenth Psalm, "The Lord is my rock, my fortress, and my savior; my God is my rock, in whom I find protection. He is my shield, the power that saves me, and my place of safety."

A commotion suddenly broke out in the streets before her, a mob of refugees fighting with a band of armed men. "Give me that goat!" a man growled, trying to wrestle an animal from a refugee. Elsewhere, men armed with spears began robbing refugees. Those who fought back were beaten.

"You cannot take our things!" a woman cried from the ground after being robbed and thrown down.

"Orders of the Guardian of Paris!" the robber growled. "All refugees have to pay to earn their keep."

Another man struggled with two ruffians clawing at his clothes. “Give us the cloak, old man!”

“Off with you!” the man shouted. “Leave me be!”

“Stop! Stop immediately!” cried Genevieve. Her voice rang out sharply like a silver trumpet. She stepped back, surprised by the strength of her voice.

The robber looked up, and seeing her religious veil, scoffed. “It’s just a sister. Ignore her.”

“I am Genevieve,” she called, “and as the Lord lives, you will heed me!”

The robbers paused again when they heard her name, looking the famed woman over dismissively.

“This city is under the protection of the Church and the Bishop of Paris,” she continued. “We are a Christian people. We will not tolerate this lawlessness!”

“Whose gonna stop us? You?” they mocked.

“The Lord sees you!” she cried out. “God will punish you for such evil.”

“God has abandoned us,” a new voice said coldly.

Everyone turned.

“Spread out!” the robbers yelled. “The Guardian is here!”

A tall man in scale mail and swathed in a black cloak made his way through the crowd. He carried a barbarian longsword at his waist. The man was middle aged, balding in the front save for a singular tuft of hair. His face was worn and wrinkled with gray stubble grown over a pock-marked chin.

“I knew we’d have to deal with the famous saint of Paris sooner or later,” said the Guardian, strolling up to Genevieve.

“I never claimed to be—”

"—spare me your false humility. You've got no power anymore. Can't you see what's happening?" He turned to the rest of the gathered crowd. "Can't you all see? It's not just Paris. Christian Rome is falling. The Franks are swarming over Gaul like ants."

"We've been threatened before," said Genevieve. "And we have survived. We always do."

"But now there's no Aetius to save you," the Guardian sneered. "No noble Victorinus to go down fighting to protect you. The power of Rome is spent. Nobody is coming to save you. There's a new order rising—an order not based on the platitudes of a dying god but on raw power," he said, clenching his gloved fist.

"And I suppose you think you are that power?" Genevieve said.

"Who is there to lead Paris? That weakling bishop?"

Genevieve shook her head. "I'm not here to debate the shortcomings of Pallus. You can imagine you are whoever you wish, but stop robbing these poor refugees. We will not stand for it."

The Guardian stepped closer—uncomfortably close. "And what are you going to do about it? You are a weak, little woman, and worse, a fraud. I knew you were a fraud from the first time I saw you."

She took a step back. "Have we met before?"

The man cracked a wry smile. Genevieve gasped. She suddenly recognized the man. "You . . . you are Desiderius. I . . . I saw you in Bishop Vivianus's council. You are the man who tried to have me drowned! You should be in prison for attempted murder!"

The Guardian scoffed. "*Attempted* murder? What is that, anyway? How can I be guilty of a crime I didn't actually commit? Do they hand out awards for *attempted* archery? I don't think so."

"You monster! You are entirely unrepentant! To think that you fell from the sacred dignity of the priesthood to this. It's shameful!"

"I woke up," the Guardian said, thumping his chest. "Why don't you? There's still time." He stepped so close his forehead was practically touching Genevieve's. He reached up and brushed her cheek with his fingers. "After all, you're still a fine-looking woman . . ."

THWACK!!

The slap could be heard from a mile away, the crack of Genevieve's hand on his face reverberating up and down the street. The crowd gasped.

"Keep your vile hands off me!" she growled. "Is it not enough that you betray your sacred priesthood and turn to villainy that you try to commit sacrilege as well?"

The slap had taken the Guardian completely off guard. He stumbled back, massaging his flushed face, wiping at the blood on his lip. His men stood dumbfounded. Sister Floriana and a group of Genevieve's women emerged from the crowd, clustering around her, staring down the Guardian with looks that could freeze the very fires of hell.

The Guardian tried to regain his composure. He flicked at the blood on his lip with his tongue and smirked at the sisters. "Ah, the army of women is here to save Paris with their prayers."

"That to God it would be so," said Genevieve.

The Guardian pointed at her. "Just stay out of my way." Then turning to his men, "Let's go!" The Guardian and his band moved out. As soon as he was gone, Genevieve crumpled up into the arms of her sisters, trembling violently.

Refugees mobbed the sisters. "Thank you, Genevieve!" they cried. The mass of people surrounded the tiny circle of sisters, reaching their hands out in hopes of touching the famous woman. "God bless you, Genevieve!" they called. Genevieve buried her head in the shoulder of one of her sisters, struggling to control her shaking. The sisters tried to form a circle around her, but she could still feel the grasping fingers of the refugees on her garments—dozens of hands touching her in hopes of . . . *something*.

"Back away!" shouted Floriana. "Genevieve needs to rest! Give us leave!" But her words were drowned out by the greater shouts of the multitude grasping and clawing at Genevieve.

"Sweet Jesus!" a peasant woman suddenly cried. "I'm healed! It's a miracle! The tumor on my neck, it's gone! It just vanished when I touched Genevieve's tunic!"

The woman's family swarmed about her, examining her neck, while even more rushed toward Genevieve, hands held out. "A miracle!" the woman kept shouting.

"What is she saying?" asked Genevieve. "I don't understand."

"I have no idea," said Floriana, shaking her head, flustered beyond hope. "But we have to get you out of here."

The sisters took Genevieve under their arms and dragged her to the side of the street. The refugee horde followed in a swarm, mothers holding up their children in hopes that Genevieve might so much as look in their direction.

"A miracle!" the woman and her family continued to shout behind the crowd.

"They're not letting up," cried one of the sisters. "At this rate, we'll be trampled to death!" When they discovered they could no longer move up the street, Floriana and Genevieve huddled beside a stone building, the former supporting the latter in her arms, the other sisters circling around them to form a human shield.

"Saint Genevieve! Saint Genevieve!" the crowd chanted. "Let us see Genevieve!"

A troupe of horsemen came thundering up the street. "Clear the road! Clear the road!" they shouted.

"Oh, thank God!" cried Floriana. "It's the bishop's men." The crowd scattered at the approach of the horses.

"Pallus sent us to fetch you," called one of the horsemen. "I'll get Genevieve back to the abbey."

"God bless you," Genevieve said weakly.

The sisters helped lift Genevieve onto the horse. When she was raised up, it became apparent how badly the crowd had swarmed her. Her tunic was torn, her skin and face scratched. The rider dashed off toward the cathedral, her arms wrapped around his torso. Snow began to fall as the chill from the rush of wind blistered her face.

Genevieve sat upon her straw mattress, her feet in a basin of warm water. She had two furs draped over her, but she still shook as several sisters attended to her in the abbey.

"Here, Mother," one said, handing her a steaming cup.

"The Lord reward you, Sister Helena," she said, taking the cup into her chilled hands. She mouthed a blessing quietly, made the sign of the cross, and drank deeply from the broth.

"How do you feel, Mother?" said Floriana.

"Oh, just a little cold and tired. But I am not worried about my body. It is my spirit that is troubled."

"How so?" the sister asked.

"No, no," Genevieve said dismissively. "I don't want to burden you with such things."

"No, please tell us!" begged Floriana.

"Yes, Mother Genevieve, tell us!" the other sisters implored.

"Oh, very well," Genevieve relented with a smile. The sisters sat down on the floor before Genevieve's bed like children arranged for story time.

"My spirit is troubled because I foresee things are going to be very difficult for us. Until today, I kept nursing hope that the situation in the empire would improve—that our trials were only temporary setbacks, that eventually stability would return. But if I am honest with myself, I know in my heart it cannot be so. We have come too far. Too much has happened. There comes a point when you simply cannot go back."

Genevieve paused, fidgeting her fingers around the cup of broth. The sisters waited quietly.

"The city is falling into chaos," she continued. "This man I saw today, the one who calls himself the Guardian of Paris, he is my old nemesis, Desiderius."

The sisters gasped. "Desiderius? Is this not the man who tried to have you drowned when you were young?"

"He is sure to cause mischief," Genevieve said. "I fear not for myself, but I worry that he may harm one of you to try to strike at me."

Her voice trembled at the thought of the sisters being injured. She remembered the feel of his icy fingers on her cheek and grimaced in visible disgust.

"We will be careful, mother!" they protested.

"We will all need to be careful. We have been accustomed to thinking of the Franks of Visigoths as the danger, but today I saw that there can be a more sinister danger right in our very midst. We must watch out for one another; we only go out in groups from now on. Every one of you is your sister's keeper. And most importantly, we must pray fervently for God to preserve us in the midst of this present evil, even as He saved Noah and his family during the flood."

The sisters nodded in agreement.

Genevieve looked out the window of her cell. The gray winter clouds were spread like a fluffy blanket across the sky. She smiled. "When I was young, I used to have a place I would go, me and some of the other girls in my village. It was a grove up on the slope of Mont-Valérien. We called it the Green Circle. It was our refuge. A lovely place—there were silver firs and abelia and flowering maple shrubs all about. You should have seen it when the sun would hit it just so in the afternoon! We read there, prayed there, spoke of our dreams. It was like a little Garden of Eden."

The women smiled at the picture Genevieve painted in their minds.

"But there is no lasting Eden on this earth," Genevieve said somberly. "In that same grove, I buried my parents when

I was a girl, just before I came here to Paris." Genevieve's eyes watered. "No lasting Eden," she repeated, sniffling. "For many of you, this abbey has been like a little Eden. You've come from all over Gaul to form a community here, to consecrate yourselves to God and to serve Christ in faith. Thus far, we've had peace. But the days are coming when God will require you to do things that tax your endurance. You will see suffering in a way you've never seen before. You won't be able to hide from it. There will be no refuge, no earthly Eden. You will have to confront the evil and suffering of this world with the same rawness Christ did when He went to the cross."

"When will these things come to us?" asked Sister Helena.

Genevieve turned to her with soft eyes. "They are already upon us."

The sisters looked at one another, distressed.

"Why must this happen now?" one of the sisters asked. "Why should we have to be the victims of such evil times?"

"Do not think like that, child!" Genevieve insisted. "We must not think of ourselves as victims! What good comes from that? What does that even mean? Why did my parents die of the plague? Why did Duke Victorinus die when we needed him most? Why was Anna's husband killed by the Franks? Why was Floriana's mother sold into slavery or Sister Marcia's brother drowned on the Seine? If you start dwelling on these agonies, all you'll see is darkness. I'm a victim, you're a victim, she's a victim—everybody is a victim! Victims of sin. That's the *only* real victimhood."

The sisters hung onto every word. They seldom heard Genevieve speak like this, and they were eager to remember.

"But thank God that's not the end of the story," said Genevieve, smiling. "Every sin is just an occasion for God's victory, and every struggle is just another adventure in the service of Christ. 'My peace I give you,' Our Lord said. There is no Eden on this earth—save for the Eden you carry in your heart. My dear sisters, come close to me, let us all pledge before the Lord to the best of our abilities that whatever comes, we will cling to Christ and keep his peace alive in our hearts, even if it is extinguished everywhere else."

"We will," said the sisters, many of them teary eyed. They scooted closer to Genevieve's bed, some even resting their heads upon her lap. Even though Genevieve was right—that there could ultimately be no lasting Eden on this earth—nevertheless, Eden truly appeared in her cell that afternoon, even if just for a fleeting moment.

Chapter 9

A Desperate Plan

It all came to pass as Genevieve had foretold. The herding of the entire rural population behind the walls of Paris became commonplace as the Franks slowly overtook the countryside. The constant evacuations made it increasingly difficult for the farmers to maintain their lands, and with each passing year, more fields went fallow as the countryfolk abandoned their farmsteads for the safety of the city. These lands were taken over by Franks, who reformed the countryside in their own image. Burly Frankish warriors squatted in the old Roman villages and grazed their horses on Roman fields. Frankish chieftains sat in dim, torchlit halls, singing and drinking to their fallen heroes while the crumbled stone buildings where Roman magistrates once sat were consumed by the wilderness. And in gloomy forest groves, the Franks worshiped their strange gods in the evening mist while the name of Christ slowly disappeared from the land.

Paris had become a Christian island in the midst of a pagan sea, but conditions inside were no less chaotic. Overcrowded and filthy, poverty was rife among the destitute throngs of Paris, and food was scarce. The well-to-do had long since fled south, retreating from the Frankish frontier and taking their wealth with them. Control of the city was a kind of negotiated truce between the Bishop of Paris and various warlords, including Desiderius the "Guardian," with each sect controlling different neighborhoods of the city. The sects imposed even heavier burdens on the populace, stealing from them, plundering their food stores, and occasionally murdering each other in the streets.

These years were difficult for Genevieve. As she had predicted, Desiderius struck out at her. Despite its proximity to Saint Etienne's Cathedral, he managed to seize control of the abbey where Genevieve had her convent. The sisters were forced out, and the building turned into a tavern. They were compelled to live in an abandoned warehouse on the other side of the Seine. The Guardian constantly hindered Genevieve's efforts to distribute food to the poor. Supplies meant to be given away as charity were seized and resold at exorbitant prices; any sisters who fought back were manhandled and driven off.

Then one autumn day, the news came: Rome had fallen. Not a Roman army or a Roman general, but the very government of the empire itself. The barbarian warlord Odoacer had captured Ravenna and forced the boy-emperor Romulus Augustulus to abdicate. Rather than claim the imperial title for himself, Odoacer sent the imperial insignia back to Constantinople, telling them the West no longer needed an emperor. Long disintegrating, Roman authority had finally disappeared in the West.

When she heard the news, Genevieve came storming into the cathedral chapel, struggling to keep her composure. She flung herself on her knees in front of the altar and held up her hands, her palms red and blistered. Just that morning, one of the Guardian's men had wrenched a wagon of grain from her hands as she attempted to hand it out to the poor. She refused to let go, but the man was too strong. Her wounded hands were evidence of her struggle. "Lord," she pleaded, "what are we going to do now? I need help! I can't so much as distribute grain from a wagon without it getting fouled up. But with the news today . . ." She looked at her skin, cracked and raw. "Dear God, I feel like we're being overwhelmed. The devil is running amok!"

If it was the devil, his work only intensified. No sooner had word reached Gaul of the emperor's abdication than Childeric, King of the Franks, began gathering his forces to march on Paris. Since she was a little girl, Genevieve had watched the Frankish menace grow. Now, they would take Paris. She recalled the words the Guardian had spoken in the street the day they met. "No one is coming to save you." She shuddered at the remembrance of his voice.

Paris was thrown into panic. Some fled the city as soon they heard, while others began squirreling their valuables away. People flooded the streets to buy supplies. Prices shot up as merchants charged a week's wages for a single sack of grain.

Within days, every bakery, granary, storehouse, and shop that sold food had been taken over by one of Paris's many factions. Two of Genevieve's sisters came rushing into the stone warehouse where the sisters were. "Mother, we were unable to obtain the supplies you sent us to purchase," said Floriana.

Sister Dalmatia stepped closer, struggling to catch her breath. "The Guardian's men are controlling access to all the food and refuse to sell it except at the most exorbitant prices. They are hoarding it all for themselves!"

"We will see about that," said Genevieve. "Come, let us go pay these gentlemen a visit."

The situation was as the sisters had said. The storehouse was being guarded by a troop of Desiderius's thugs, armed with clubs. Hungry Parisians swarmed about, pressing the men and calling for food. "Back!" barked one of the thugs, raising his club menacingly.

"Fair prices!" shouted a man as he lunged for one of the ruffians. The man was met with the *thwack* of a club over his head, sending him to the ground.

"You want food, you're gonna have to pay handsomely!" roared the leader.

"And what do you expect them to pay with?" called Genevieve. "No one is left in Paris but the poor and sick."

"Ah, it is Paris's saint," the man said smugly.

"For the love of Christ, give these people food!" Genevieve pleaded. "We will pay a fair price, but don't use the hunger of your brothers and sisters as an occasion for greed!"

The man shrugged. "Guardian's orders. This grain is being reserved for our men. Anyone who wants some is going to have to pay dearly—or try to get it by force."

Genevieve was so angry she shook. "Come, sisters," she said. "Let us take this matter to the Lord."

"You do that!" the man jeered as the sisters turned away. "See if your God will help you!"

Genevieve and her sisters gathered in the cathedral. After a prolonged time of silent prayer, Genevieve blurted out, "I will get food from the Franks." The sisters whispered among themselves, frightened and confused.

After their prayers, Genevieve and her sisters met with Bishop Urscinius. He had been in office three years and had proven to be a holy and competent man, bold but also prudent. He was worldly wise, always subordinating his wisdom to the good of souls. Urscinius listened to Genevieve's plan with great interest.

"It is clear that the city is going to fall to the Franks sooner or later," Genevieve argued. "My reputation is known among them. If I go out to them in humility, it will be a gesture of good will on the part of Paris. It may move Childeric to spare our city from fire and sword."

Urscinius considered this. "And the king may realize that relieving the starving of Paris will win the favor of the Parisians. He will win a reputation for clemency. Yes, I see the wisdom in your plan, Genevieve. But how do you propose to get to them with the city under siege?"

"If you will arrange some boats, my sisters and I will row out on the Seine under the cover of darkness. We will take the river out past the Frankish lines, then seek the king. After that, we will commend it all to God."

"Your bravery is to be admired," Urscinius said. "But still, I shall feel better about this if I send a troop of armed men with you for protection."

"No!" Genevieve protested. "I am hoping we will not be seen, but if we are discovered, the presence of armed men could lead the Franks to think we are a war party. If we go alone, there is little chance the Franks will mistake a band of unarmed women for a hostile threat."

Urscinius furled his brow. "It is risky, but I see no other option. The Guardian's men are hoarding all the food. At this rate, we will be facing starvation in days. When will you go?"

"This very night before dawn, if you can arrange it."

"Very well. I will have the boats prepared. May Christ bless your endeavors."

Genevieve and her sisters knelt before Urscinius, receiving his episcopal blessing.

Genevieve and her sisters spent the night in prayer and discussions about the plan. They slept little, too nervous for what the following day would bring. Finally, the bell tolled the quarta vigília, the fourth watch of the night. "It's time to go," said Genevieve. "May God be merciful to us."

Bearing a torch, Genevieve led the thirty sisters out to the riverfront behind the Cathedral of Saint Etienne, near the spot where Genevieve was almost drowned years ago. There the sisters found four longboats with oars tied up. They filed into the longboats under torchlight. Within minutes, the boats were gliding down the Seine, a little flotilla of sisters embarking on their dangerous mission of mercy. Genevieve's boat led the way, eight sisters manning the rows while Genevieve huddled at the stern, gray cloak draped about her little

form, sharp eyes peeled and continually scanning the shoreline like an owl scouting for prey. "Lord, grant us stealth," she whispered, plunging her torch into the water, a *sizzle* rising from the heated water.

Though dawn was hours away and the night was still thick, Parisians had begun to gather on the banks of the Seine. Word had spread about Genevieve's desperate plan, and they wanted to see the sisters off with their prayers. They knew better than to shout or call attention to the sisters; they merely lifted their hands, some holding crosses aloft. Genevieve raised her own hand in silent solidarity.

The river began to narrow. Genevieve saw the wooden bridge that marked the boundary of Paris on the Seine. Called the *ponticulus* by the locals, it spanned some forty meters across the river, held aloft by a series of posts fixed every twenty feet. The bridge was heavily fortified with palisades and towers—and on this night, thronged with Parisians. From down below, Genevieve could see their torches flicker.

Normally, the posts of the ponticulus were connected by a series of chains, preventing unwanted boats from putting in at Paris. But by arrangement of Bishop Urscinius, the chain between the two central posts had been temporarily removed, allowing Genevieve's boats to slip through. Genevieve looked up as the flotilla glided beneath the structure like floating between the legs of a giant.

Once we come out the other side, we are on our own.

Presently, the boats passed the bridge, entering open waters on the outside of the city. The river broadened again, and the rushes and little islands and sandbars that cluttered the water provided them cover. The women rowed slowly and silently, their oars making scarcely a splash as they dipped in and out of the dark water. Genevieve's knuckles were clenched, her jaw locked in anxiety. She knew this was the most desperate moment. If the Franks saw them and supposed they were a scouting party from the city, they'd be shot by archers and killed. Genevieve prayed.

O Lord, who wraps thyself in darkness as with a cloak, cover us in shadow that we may pass unseen.

It was not long before the Frankish campfires came into view, flaring along the left bank of the river, at first a few here and there but gradually increasing until they looked like a banner of stars filling the plains before Paris. Genevieve's stomach sank.

There are so many of them!

The boats hugged the opposite shore of the river, the sisters trusting their silence and the darkness of night to keep them obscured. "We have to put some distance between ourselves and the main camp before we land," Genevieve whispered to the sisters. "Steady on." The paddles continued brushing over the water, propelling the crafts silently down the black waters of the Seine until the campfires began to wane. Genevieve scanned the banks, searching for any sign of trouble.

When the camp seemed far enough behind them, Genevieve gave the word to draw the boats to shore. A band of pink light glowed on the eastern horizon as the sisters scrambled up the muddy banks and ducked under a cluster of rowan trees. "Now we must find the Paris road and head due west. Urscinius thinks King Childeric and his entourage will be coming up the road this very morning. With God's help, we will intercept him."

The sisters walked two-by-two, moving silently through the field adjacent to the river. Everything was dim and gray, save the few beams of pink that announced the coming of day. The women kept their eyes downcast, hands folded in the sleeves of their tunics while they prayed silently for the success of the mission. But not Genevieve. She was alert and on edge, continually scanning their surroundings for signs of the road—or the Franks.

Soon the field sloped downward, and at the base of the hill, Genevieve spied the dusty Paris road. "Thank God there's no one around," she said, crossing herself. The women scrambled down the hill and soon were on the road headed west. But then . . .

A detachment of a dozen Frankish cavalrymen came up the road, led by a burly captain, clean shaven save for a long mustache that flowed down his cheeks. They rode up to the sisters, who were trying not to tremble.

"What is your business?" the Frankish captain growled from atop his horse.

"I am Genevieve of Paris. My sisters and I have come to plead the case of our city before your lord, King Childeric."

"Genevieve? I have heard of you." The captain looked her up and down "Why should I trust you? What if you've come to kill the king?"

"Kill the king?" Genevieve exclaimed. "We are religious women! Sisters of Christ! We do not bear arms!"

The Frank grunted. "Spies, perhaps?"

"Spies? What spies go out in parties of thirty? And if I were a spy, why would I insist on being taken right before your master?" The Frank scratched his head, struggling to think out the contingencies Genevieve laid before him. "Please," she continued, "we merely want to throw ourselves before the king's mercy on behalf of our city."

"Very well," the Frank finally nodded. "I am called Baldric, one of the king's captains. Childeric is up the road. I can take you to him. But do not expect much for your city. The king is bringing a thousand more warriors. Paris is finished."

"I do not come to quibble about politics," said Genevieve. "I am here on a mission of mercy."

"Mercy, eh?" Baldric stroked his mustache. "Well, I will make sure you at least get to Childeric. Whether the king hears your petition or uses you for target practice is your own problem."

"We'll take the risk," Genevieve said. Her sisters looked at each other nervously. They did not fancy being used for target practice.

Baldric glanced over the sisters with a bemused look, as if unsure whether the embassy of women standing before him was some grand joke. "All right, then, let's go," he said finally. "You men, continue on your way to the city. I will join you later with the king." The horsemen nodded and continued down the Paris road, while Baldric led the women in the opposite direction.

Baldric guided the women up the road as morning broke upon the land. A cool mist settled on the path, obscuring the landscape. Occasionally, little bands of Frankish warriors would pass them like specters emerging from the mist. "Guundach!" they would greet Baldric, who would raise his hand and grunt, "Hoi!" in response. The warriors stared at the women as they passed by, trying to determine their intentions.

Genevieve kept her head down, mouthing prayers silently.

"How do we know we can trust this fellow?" whispered Dalmatia. "He could be leading us into some filthy bog to kill us."

"All things as God orders," Genevieve responded stoically. "We're in their hands now. What will be will be. Trust God."

Soon the sisters heard the sounds of a large troupe of horses ahead of them in the fog. The troupe emerged from the mist, an impressively arrayed band of mounted Frankish nobles. They all bore battle axes and had shields strapped to their backs. Each man wore the distinctive Frankish mustache, some of the biggest Genevieve had ever seen. At the head of the riders, a middle-aged man in a rough blue tunic sat erect on his horse. His mustache was the grandest of all, dipping down well beneath his chin, obscuring his mouth. He wore his hair in flowing locks down to the middle of his back. No other man had hair such as this.

"Why does he look like that?" asked Floriana.

"Frankish kings distinguish themselves by their hair," said Genevieve. "Try not to stare." Floriana nodded and looked at the ground. The other sisters followed her example.

Baldric raised his hand. "King Childeric, I present the religious woman Genevieve from the city of Paris. She and her sisters have come to you on a mission of mercy."

Childeric called his company to a halt and dismounted. "Genevieve!" he muttered in surprise. His eyes widened. "Genevieve!" he said again with a booming smile, arms extended, walking toward her.

"Lord Childeric?" she said.

The king strode up and wrapped his burly arms around her, giving her a crushing hug and lifting her off the ground. She felt her back crack as he squeezed her. The sisters covered their mouths in shock.

The king released her, and beaming with joy, took her face in his calloused hands. "It is good to see you!" he exclaimed.

"It is . . . it is good to see you as well, sire," she stammered.

He turned to his riders. "This woman gave victory to my father and the Franks in the war against the Huns. She fought with her prayers. All the Romans of Paris believed it, and I believe it, too. She is a magician!" The Franks all nodded and stroked their mustaches, impressed. Baldric looked Genevieve up and down with a newfound respect.

"I'm no magician, sir," Genevieve said softly, "but I do pray, and I seek what is good. And now I direct my petitions to you, King, on behalf of the people of Paris."

The king's smile vanished. "What of Paris?"

"My lord, the siege has brought about frightful conditions within the city. Our people are starving. I beg you to give us food so that we might not perish."

Childeric burst out in raucous laughter. His nobles mimicked him boisterously. "What king supplies food to a city he is trying to subdue?"

"You have a great opportunity here," Genevieve said. "Paris will fall sooner or later. The city will be yours, and its people will be your subjects. What better way to show your benevolence than to relieve their hunger?"

"Let them starve," one of the warriors blurted out. "If we feed them, they'll just resist longer." Many of the other warriors grunted their approval.

"But if you send us food, it will be a sign of your greatness," Genevieve continued. "The people of Paris will see you are a just man. They will not fear your rule."

"I see," said Childeric. "Do you think you can convince them to surrender the city to me?"

Genevieve was taken aback at the request. "I am only a religious sister," said Genevieve. "I cannot promise any such thing."

"But you hold sway with the people. They all hold you to be a wonderworker. Can you not persuade them to give up and open the city?"

"My lord," she said, "if you will send food into our troubled city—and give me your word that your men will treat us well when the city is taken—I swear to you I will do my best to persuade the Parisians it is in their best interest to surrender."

The king pondered Genevieve's words. Then looking to his men, called out. "Wulfram, how many wagons of grain do we have?"

An elder warrior called back, "Two dozen at least. Enough for a fortnight."

"We will send a dozen to relieve the starving of Paris," declared the king.

"Thank you, Lord Childeric!" Genevieve said, dropping to her knees and kissing the hem of the king's tunic.

"That's an entire week's worth of bread I'm taking away from my army," Childeric said. "That means I will give you one week to secure the city's surrender. If Paris does not surrender in that time, we will storm the city, and all agreements of clemency will be null."

"I understand," Genevieve said solemnly.

Childeric smiled. "I hope for your sake this plan works. But if it doesn't, at least you Parisians will die with full bellies." The Franks erupted in laughter.

"By God's grace, all things will be ordered well," said Genevieve.

"I will have you escorted back to the city to ensure you are not harmed. Wulfram will have the grain delivered at sunset. Tell your people to be ready. Clovis! Clovis, come escort these women back to Paris."

A ruddy, handsome youth appeared on horseback at the king's side. He was no more than twelve years old. "Don't be deceived by his appearance," said Childeric. "Clovis is my firstborn son. Nobody will harass you in his company."

Genevieve's eyes widened at the sight of the youth. Something about the lad struck her. She made the sign of the cross. "Afterward, he sent his son to them, saying, 'They will reverence my son,'" she mumbled.

"What's that?" the boy blurted out.

"Nothing," Genevieve said apologetically. "Just a prayer from our Scriptures. We are in your hands, Prince Clovis."

"Clovis, see them safely to the gates of Paris, then meet me outside the city at sunset," Childeric ordered.

"Yes, Father," the boy nodded. Then turning to the sisters, "Okay, you women, we move. *Now*!"

"I prefer the father," whispered Dalmatia to Floriana.

"Hush!" Floriana said.

Chapter 10

The Siege of Paris

The boy Clovis led the women back to Paris through the Frankish lines as Childeric had commanded. Genevieve found the pace brutal. Clovis—leading from horseback—made little effort to wait for the women. Falling too far behind would expose them to the voracity of the Frankish soldiers. So, the women wheezed and groaned as they trotted behind Clovis's horse, mile after mile up the road back to Paris.

Approaching the plain outside the city, they first beheld the true size of the Frankish army. The entire countryside around Paris had become a massive military camp. Cluttered with thousands of rough Frankish tents of animal hide, the fields were unrecognizable. The whole place teemed with hordes of Frankish soldiers—cooking, sharpening their axes, drinking, lounging about, waiting for the word to attack. As the Franks preferred to fight from horseback, the camp was also thronged with horses. The accumulation of the manure gave the camp a rancid, putrid smell that the women could scarcely tolerate but which the Franks seemed indifferent to. Dogs and rats scavenged about openly, rummaging through Frankish provisions and picking over heaps of waste. The sight and smell of the Frankish hordes was unlike anything Genevieve had ever witnessed. As she jogged, she could feel her body shaking from the thought of this host swarming over Paris.

Once Clovis led them into the camp, he slackened his pace considerably, as he was stopped by countless war chiefs seeking to speak with him. Genevieve and the others had no choice but to stand exposed in the midst of the camp while Clovis chatted with his Franks.

"All morning he keeps us running like a pack of animals through the countryside, and now in this awful place, he pauses and makes us wait?" lamented Dalmatia.

"Do not show fear," said Genevieve calmly. "It will only embolden them."

Indeed, a large group of Frankish warriors had begun to gather around the women. They maintained some distance, seeing they were in the company of Clovis—but even so, their mustachioed gazes unnerved the women. The Franks recognized no vow of chastity and thought little of human life.

A Frank lunged forward and tore the veil from Genevieve's head. He waved it about in the air to the laughter of his comrades. Other Franks began lunging at the women, trying to steal their veils. The women shrieked and swatted at them, as if trying to fight off a swarm of insects—massive, hairy insects. Genevieve shook uncontrollably, worse than when she was a young child and fell into the Seine in February.

"The Lord is my shepherd, I shall not want," she mouthed. She bit her lip to halt its trembling and hid her hands within the sleeves of her tunic.

"Cease your petty games!" Clovis barked. "These women are under my father's protection!"

The laughter faded as the men backed away in deference to Clovis's command—although without returning the veils. Genevieve took a deep breath and crossed herself. Clovis watched her, then said, "Let's go."

The little party continued through the Frankish lines without further incident. As they approached the city, they entered the no man's land between the Frankish encampment and the city walls, a little shy of a quarter mile of open ground. The Franks had stayed back to avoid arrows fired from the Parisian ramparts. The boy-prince bid them farewell at the edge of the encampment before the empty ground. "You go now," he directed. "May your God be with you. Expect the supplies before sunset. You women are bold. I hope you survive."

"We would like that very much as well," Genevieve said, bowing. With that, Clovis turned and disappeared into the thousands of other mounted warriors within the Frankish camp.

At the approach of Genevieve's party, the city gates were cracked open, and the women hustled inside. The news they bore was received with great rejoicing, and the Parisians hailed Genevieve as a heroine and savior of the city. Childeric was true to his word—that afternoon, after his entourage arrived in camp, Wulfram personally led a troupe of Franks to deliver the promised grain to the city gates. Before departing, however, the gnarled Frankish warrior repeated the terms of Childeric: that the city should be granted seven days to surrender before being stormed.

Predictably, as soon as the grain was delivered, Desiderius and his goons showed up at the city gates to confiscate it. Urscinius, however, had prepared for this and assembled a militia of faithful Catholic men to guard the wagons. Though armed only with rude spears, meat cleavers, and mallets, their sheer numbers gave Desiderius pause. Urscinius himself stood by the men, urging them to resist the advance of Desiderius. For a moment, there was a tense standoff, Desiderius and his armed thugs facing the band of Urscinius's militia spread out in a semicircle around the grain wagons. Genevieve and her sisters, too, stood tall with the men, facing down the voracious Guardian.

Desiderius scowled at Genevieve, his pock-marked face downcast. The people of Paris had become desperate, and desperate people are dangerous. Desiderius evidently decided not to risk confrontation. "Come, men, leave them to their grain. We have what we need." The goons disappeared and the situation defused. The people swarmed Genevieve in gratitude, cheering and lifting her and the sisters upon their shoulders while Urscinius saw to the equitable distribution of grain.

True to her word, Genevieve urged the surrender of Paris to Childeric and proclaimed the grain delivery as a sign of the

Frankish king's good faith. But Desiderius urged the Parisians to fight. Suddenly fancying himself a protector of Parisian liberties, Desiderius seemed to appear on every square and corner, boldly calling the men of Paris to battle. "The Franks already think we are weak!" he cried. "If we make no stand, offer them no resistance, what sort of rule will they have over us? They will abuse us and make us their slaves! We must fight!"

Genevieve was beside herself. She and her sisters related the words of Childeric, arguing that the only safety was in submission. But the fear and loathing of the Franks was too great; the Romans of Gaul considered the Franks brutal barbarians and could not be persuaded to yield to them. To make matters worse, Bishop Urscinius vacillated, seeming to support Genevieve's position but also unwilling to publicly call for surrender to Childeric. Meanwhile, Desiderius had organized the able-bodied men of the city into a militia. Whereas before he had been an avaricious hoarder of food, now he was as generous as he had been greedy. He opened the storehouses and gave liberally, winning many men to his side. And to all who would listen, he calumniated Genevieve as a traitor for arguing surrender.

By the eve of the sixth day after her return, it was clear that the Parisians meant to fight. When all that could be done had been done, she and the women withdrew to the cathedral with the bishop to keep prayerful vigil. The militia, under the guidance of Desiderius, positioned their forces at the walls about the western gates, where the concentration of Frankish forces was greatest.

The battle was a disaster. The Franks surged against the wooden palisade like a flood, throwing the Parisian defenders into terror. The militiamen fired harmless arrows from the walls before fleeing in fear and confusion as the Frankish forces swelled. Making matters worse, Desiderius and his captains disappeared as the Parisians withdrew from the wall. Nobody could find them in the chaos, and the defenders were left without guidance.

Genevieve and her sisters stayed within the confines of Saint Etienne's, praying continually in shifts. The church teemed with families seeking sanctuary, though Genevieve doubted the Franks would respect the sacred precincts. Kneeling before the altar, she pressed against sobbing women and frightened children, clutching their hands while leading them in the recitation of the Beatitudes.

The city's fall was swift. The Parisians did not fight well enough to hold off the collapse, but they fought just enough to let the Franks know they did not hand the city over willingly. The main gates were forced with little effort, the wooden ramparts and the gatehouse torched. There was a horrific period of indiscriminate slaughter as the Frankish cavalry poured through the streets, slaying all they encountered. Genevieve could hear the trampling of Frankish horses in the streets outside; she discerned the harsh, guttural cries of their warriors calling to one another.

Only the bridge over the Seine separates them from us, thought Genevieve. *All they must do is ride across the bridge, and we are done.*

"Lord, spare your people!" she pleaded, head bowed upon the flagstone of the sanctuary. Fortunately, Childeric had given orders to respect the sanctity of the church, apparently out of admiration for Genevieve. The people gathered in Saint Etienne's remained unharmed—for now.

The pillage soon gave way to a more ordered occupation as Childeric and his entourage entered the city to the cheers of the Franks. Childeric ordered the entire population of Paris to be rounded up and herded out to the plains outside the city. The Parisians were instructed to bring all their valuables with them. Those who had something to pay would be turned loose; those who did not were likely to be enslaved.

"Oh, Mother, what is going to happen to us?" Floriana cried, clasping the hem of Genevieve's tunic.

Genevieve locked arms with her. "I do not know, dear daughter, but let us face it together." The other sisters joined as well, locking elbows and processing out on the bridge across the Seine to join the throngs being driven like cattle outside the walls. Bishop Urscinius followed behind in full episcopal vestments, hands folded in prayer, leading the clergy in singing the Lamentations of Jeremiah. Crowds of Parisians followed, heads bowed in humility, mumbling their own rustic prayers or simply crossing their hands in a silent act of simple piety.

The October day was bright, but the winter chill was already setting in, a wind gust blowing up off the plains, numbing Genevieve's fingers. The long train of prisoners were marched out of the charred gates onto the plain turned into a muddy pit from the tromping of thousands of Frankish men and horses. They were taken some ways from the city before being forced to line up. The Parisians were downcast and quiet, save for the wailing of cold and hungry children and the hushes of their mothers attempting to silence them. The walls of Paris smoldered in the distance, the smoke of their ruin ascending like a black serpent twirling into the blue vault of heaven.

The Franks began to gather around the prisoners, eyeing them up and down while their captains discussed how many would be allotted to whom. Genevieve again felt the sense of being exposed—of sitting as a kind of prey in the midst of the predatory Franks. They were human chattel, spoils of war to be distributed as the Franks saw fit.

The shakedown began. The Franks, with little order, plowed into the rows of prisoners, seizing the Parisians violently and rummaging about their bags and pockets for any items of value. Rings, jewelry, linens, bracelets, coins were all seized. The fate of those who had no valuables varied; sometimes they were simply tossed aside, others were dragged off to be enslaved, depending on the whims of the Franks.

By dusk, the Franks had begun drinking, and the situation grew considerably worse. Frankish soldiers abused their captives for amusement. Genevieve saw a man who could not pay bashed over the head with a drinking vase while the Franks laughed and clapped. When they saw some of the captives had gold teeth, they held down these unfortunate wretches and yanked the gold from their mouths with a pair of pliers. The Parisians began to panic, cowering before their captors. Like animals sinking into a killing frenzy, the Franks sensed the fear, smelling it like a scent, which only increased their brutality.

As a religious, Genevieve and the other sisters had no valuables, meaning they were mostly left alone by the Franks, left to sit on a small hillock by themselves. As darkness began to fall, though, a troop of drunken Franks took notice of the sisters and came toward them menacingly.

"We are consecrated to God," Genevieve called to them. "We have no valuables."

"You've got what I want!" a burly warrior growled back, seizing Sister Dalmatia by the arm and dragging her off. Dalmatia screamed.

"Unhand her!" Genevieve yelled.

The other Franks laughed. "Would you look at that? Leudagar said he needed a wife! Who'd have thought he'd find one tonight!"

"Help me!" screamed Dalmatia, squirming about in Leudagar's iron grip.

Genevieve rushed forward. "Take your hands off her! She is a spouse of Jesus Christ!"

"Not anymore," Leudagar said, laughing. "She's a spouse of mine!"

"Childeric said we were not to be harmed!" insisted Genevieve, beating upon the Frank's broad shoulders with her fists.

Leudagar whirled about with astonishing speed and slapped Genevieve with the back of his gnarled hand. Blood filled her mouth as she reeled to the ground, face burning. "Well, Childeric ain't around, is he?" Leudagar barked. Genevieve could smell the ale on his foul breath. "C'mon, lads! Let's go find Theudric and the rest of the boys." He heaved Dalmatia upon his shoulder as one carries a sack of flour and trudged off. She sobbed and beat her little fists upon the Frank's back,

but it was of no avail; she might as well be pounding against a boulder. She disappeared into the darkness.

"This is madness," Genevieve said, fighting back tears. "I'm going to find Childeric this instant!"

She stormed off in a fury to find the King of the Franks. The remaining sisters trailed behind, calling out and begging her to stay put. But righteous indignation brimmed within Genevieve. She would not be dissuaded.

All over the camp, similar barbarities were being inflicted upon the Parisians: women were being carried off, prisoners abused, and any who resisted were beaten or even killed. As she passed through the camp, she saw a clearing where some clergy were being manhandled by the Franks.

Good heavens! Could this be Urscinius or one of the priests?

Drawing closer, she saw that the Franks had compelled some poor clergyman to stand against a horse post with a jug upon his head. He was tied to the post around his neck so he could not move away. The drunken Franks hurled their hand axes at the target, attempting to knock the jug off the wretched man's head. The lifeless bodies of two other priests at the foot of the post was a testimony to the Franks' poor aim. The priest was quaked, the jug jostling atop his head.

A Frankish warrior hurled an ax at the jug. It sailed past the man's head, missing him by a few inches. "Blast! Stand still, priest!" the Frank barked, taking a swig of ale.

"Who is that priest?" Genevieve said to herself. He looked familiar. She moved a little closer into the torchlight. "Good Lord! Desiderius!"

Desiderius looked up. His eyes locked with Genevieve's. A look of desperation swept over him. "Genevieve! For the love of God, Genevieve, help me!" he cried aloud.

Why is he dressed like a priest?

It took Genevieve a moment to put it all together. When it had become clear the city was going to fall, Desiderius went back to his clerical garment, hoping to disguise himself.

"Genevieve!" he called again.

A large Frank with a thick blond mustache stood up. "Shut your mouth!" he roared. Then taking an ax, he threw it at the jug. It thudded into the horse post only a few inches above Desiderius's head.

Genevieve thrust herself into the clearing. "Stop this! You must stop this!" she cried. "You're going to kill him!"

"So?" one of the Franks grunted. "We already killed a few," another said, nodding to the bodies at Desiderius's feet.

"Where is Childeric?" Genevieve demanded. "I insist you take me to him."

"He's gone on and left things to me to clean up here," said the voice of a boy. Genevieve turned. Prince Clovis emerged from the shadows, ax in one hand and a jug of beer in the other.

Genevieve threw herself at his feet. "Prince, I beg you, stop the barbarities your men are inflicting upon our people! Your father gave his word that we would be treated well!"

"*If* you surrendered peacefully," said Clovis. "You didn't. We gave you grain, and you still fought back. And now the boys want to have a little fun."

Another ax hurled at Desiderius, whizzing past his head and thudding in the grass behind him. The Franks jeered.

"Please, grant me this priest's life!" Genevieve pleaded. "You want gold? I can get you gold. Name your price."

"Get her out of here!" one the Franks bellowed. "She's ruining our fun!"

"I beg you," she continued, undeterred, "your father heeded my words; show yourself to be a true son of Childeric! This man is a priest; I am a sister. Please let me take him out of here."

"Oh, God! Thank you, Genevieve, thank you!" blubbered Desiderius.

The young prince looked at Desiderius, staring blankly for a moment. "I haven't taken a throw yet," he said coldly. The Frankish warriors roared their approval as the young prince stepped into the clearing.

"Clovis, please! Turn him loose!" said Genevieve.

Clovis ignored her, taking another swig of his ale, then, tossing the jug aside, took his ax in both hands.

"Please, for the love of God . . ." Genevieve made the sign of the cross.

The Frankish prince launched the ax through the air.

A sickening crunch.

The Franks cheered and stamped their feet. "Right in the head! Did you see that?"

Desiderius's body convulsed as blood drained down his arms and pooled about the foot of the post.

Clovis turned to Genevieve. "Like I said, the boys need a bit of fun. Better luck next time."

Genevieve collapsed. She ripped the veil from her head, pressed her brow into the grimy earth, tore her hair and screamed—a scream of such force as to startle the burly

Frankish warriors, a scream that contained within it all the sorrow of a lifetime, taking Genevieve back to the cold tombs of her parents in Nanterre and bringing her all the way to the present moment, a singularly bold and desperate cry against all the injustices of life, a scream that made the demons tremble, and whose supplication pierced the very halls of heaven.

Genevieve fell silent. The Franks looked on, stunned at the raw power that had just escaped from this woman. Her sisters caught up with her, emerging into the clearing just in time to see the strange sight. Even Clovis was surprised. He knelt beside the trembling woman and picked up her veil from the dirt. The boy took Genevieve's hand and put the veil in her quivering palm. Genevieve sat up, gazing with a tear-streaked face at the prince looking down upon her. She returned the veil to her head, shrouding again the bright blond hair which had been momentarily exposed, save the two braids that ever flanked her cheeks.

A wry smile wound across Clovis's face. "All right, boys," he said, "I think we've had enough fun. Tell the captains to let all the prisoners go now."

Chapter 11

They Return with Shouts of Joy

The Parisians gradually filtered back into the city over the next few days, though they found it greatly changed. The grander buildings had been given over to the chieftains of Childeric for their use, while many lesser structures had been burned or sacked. With the death of Desiderius, Genevieve was able to move out of the warehouse and back into the convent. She found the cathedral and surrounding buildings completely pillaged: sacred vessels, vestments, tapestries, and anything of value had been seized by the avaricious Franks. Thankfully, though, the buildings themselves remained undamaged, allowing her to restore some vestige of ordinary religious life in the convent.

Control of the town was given over to one of Childeric's chiefs, named Folmar, who assumed for himself the old Roman title *dux*. The thought of a mustachioed Frankish warlord taking the title once used by the noble Victorinus made Genevieve wince. But there were more pressing matters to worry about, namely, that this Folmar was holding

Bishop Urscinius hostage, refusing to release him until the Christians of Paris paid a hefty ransom. Once again, Paris was without a bishop. And as the Christian people had just been fleeced of all their valuables, the likelihood of this ransom coming anytime soon was remote.

As fall progressed, life slowly returned to normal, albeit a different normal. Folmar maintained a large retinue in the city so that the Franks became a common sight upon Parisian streets. Burned-out buildings were slowly rebuilt but in the rusticated style of the Franks, making the town feel more like a Frankish outpost than an old Roman city. The refugees who had swelled Paris during the siege returned to their farms, finding them completely looted or inhabited by squatting Frankish warriors who claimed them as spoils of war. In these cases, the Franks allowed them to return to their farmsteads only as servants, working their former lands under the command of the Franks and turning over part of their harvest as taxes.

The religious situation fared somewhat better, though still delicate. Having plundered Saint Etienne's, the Franks cared little for the cathedral and left the Christians to their worship. Occasionally, the Franks would wander in, gaze about the sanctuary in silent curiosity, then meander out. Regular liturgies were restored under the administration of the archdeacon until the bishop was restored. Christians came to and from Mass quietly, minding their own affairs and trying not to provoke their Frankish overlords. The Franks were not necessarily hostile to Christianity, but Genevieve noticed they lacked propriety when it came to sacred things. It was best to keep demonstrations of the faith modest so as not to incite them to acts of sacrilege—a priest who tried to reprimand a gang of Franks for their public drunkenness was tossed into a cart of horse dung; another who went out wearing his clerical stole had it ripped from his body and used as a handkerchief.

Genevieve tried to accommodate, but she could find no ease in the new situation. Her heart was sick. In her prayers, she continually saw the image of Sister Dalmatia being heaved off into the night upon the shoulders of that Frankish brute, Leudagar. What was her fate? She lamented, too, the captivity of Bishop Urscinius. And tears streaked down her face as she recalled the scores of husbands or wives, hundreds of them, whose spouses had been taken away as slaves. She shuddered thinking of the Parisian children so suddenly and cruelly deprived of their parents.

For the time, she could do nothing but pray, every day, as the weather turned colder, and a somber Christmas rolled past. The burden for the lost Parisians only grew as time went by until finally Genevieve could ignore it no longer.

On the Feast of Epiphany, Genevieve sat down at her writing table by candlelight, rubbed her stiff fingers to warm them, and put pen to parchment. The letter, addressed to King Childeric, was a torrent of complaints about the situation of her beloved Paris under the rule of the Franks. She lamented the poor manners of the Frankish occupiers, the sad state of the Church without Bishop Urscinius, and the continued heartbreak over so many captives carried off as Frankish prisoners.

I plead, by the blood of Christ and the kindness I believe is in your heart, use your authority to rectify these wrongs and show yourself just in the eyes of the Christians.

She quickly scrawled her name across the bottom—"Genevieve of Paris."

For several weeks, there came no response. This did not surprise Genevieve. She questioned whether or not Childeric even had someone literate in his court in Tournai who could read the letter to him. And if he did, why should this brute brooding in his shadowy halls care what a Christian woman in Paris thought?

But then one day, early in the season of Lent, Urscinius came stumbling into the cathedral during vespers, ragged and thin but in good spirits. He fell to his knees and bowed his head before the altar. "Praise God!" he cried. Genevieve and the others turned and looked, wondering what the disturbance was all about. They nearly cried when he explained that orders had come down from Childeric, ordering Folmar, in the strongest possible terms, to turn the bishop loose immediately.

Nor was this the only marvel, for in the following days, Parisian men and women given up for lost began straggling back into the city. Across Paris, there were happy reunions of husbands, wives, parents, and children. All of them told a similar story of being carried off into enslavement after the fall of Paris, but King Childeric, at the behest of Genevieve, had encouraged his men to turn their slaves loose. For a full week, visitors turned up at the abbey to thank Genevieve for their freedom, bringing loaves of bread, flower garlands, or other tokens of gratitude. Routinely, she would rise at dawn for Lauds to find baskets of food and gifts already accumulated at the abbey gates. The sight of these humble offerings stirred Genevieve's soul. "Those who sow in tears reap with shouts of joy," she said, crossing herself. "They go forth weeping, bearing the seed for sowing, but they return with shouts of joy, bearing their sheaves with them."

Some weeks later, a young woman walked into the abbey gardens, draped in a thick cloak and a rag of unkept, dark hair, her countenance sunken by exhaustion. Genevieve looked up from her gardening, squinting at the visitor, who looked more familiar the closer she got. She studied her more intently until joy filled her heart. "Dalmatia!" She flocked to the young woman, throwing her arms around her. The other sisters dropped their gardening and rushed to the girl as well, pressing upon her and hugging her through their tears. Genevieve took the young sister's face in her hands and kissed her forehead. "I barely recognized you without your veil! I prayed for you every day! Oh, dearest Dalmatia! You were dead, and now you are alive again! You were lost and are found!"

Dalmatia at first only stared. Then, lip quivering, fell upon Genevieve's shoulder and balled. "Oh, Mother!"

"It's okay, child, you're home now," Genevieve said, stroking her hair.

"Mother," Dalmatia sniffled—then stepping back, she parted her cloak, revealing a full, round belly—"I am with child." The sisters fell silent as they stared at the plump womb. Genevieve felt a mixture of sadness, compassion, and horror at what the young woman must have gone through. "Mother, have I sinned?" Dalmatia asked, trembling. "Will God cast me out?"

"No, Sister, no!" exclaimed Genevieve. She again pulled the young woman to her, and again Dalmatia dissolved into a mass of tears upon Genevieve's shoulder. "Don't worry, dear one," said Genevieve. "We will figure something out."

The sisters again closed in upon their companion, linking arms around the two in a ring of protection. Like much about those chaotic days, Dalmatia's return both consoled and challenged the sisters.

Dalmatia was housed with a generous Christian widow of Paris. That summer, she gave birth to a son, whom she called Deodatus, meaning the "gift of God." Though the duties of motherhood precluded her from partaking in the religious regimen of the abbey, Dalmatia and her son were regular fixtures there over the coming years. The boy was raised on the knees of Genevieve, who came to love the child as her own. Deodatus grew into a towheaded boy of bubbling exuberance, eager for adventure. Genevieve would sit in the gardens in the afternoon sun, praying the Psalms and watching the boy play about the abbey grounds, swinging his stick at imaginary foes. She would smile at his innocence, recalling her own youth as a barefoot country child tromping about the fields around Nanterre.

As for Duke Folmar, he and his men were deeply impressed at the influence Genevieve had exercised over Childeric. He began to understand the important role Genevieve and the sisters played in the community and treated them accordingly. Their manners gradually improved. Though there was no way to retrieve the items pillaged from the church during the sack of the town, Folmar gave a considerable sum to Urscinius, allowing the bishop to replace most of what was stolen. In time, the Franks came to hold the clergy in a kind of superstitious reverence, leading to the eradication of sacrilegious assaults against them.

Years passed. King Childeric died, and the young Prince Clovis was acclaimed King of the Franks. Clovis grew into a strong young man, with his own blond mustache sprouting from his upper lip. He had his own battles, like his father, and things went on in the world much as they always had. Genevieve passed into middle age, her once delicate hands showing the first signs of wrinkles, and crow's feet appeared around her eyes. In the morning when she cleaned herself in solitude and removed her veil, she saw her blond hair graced by emerging streaks of gray. It flowed down her braids, like strands of silver intricately woven among the blond.

In the year 493, the Church of Paris was honored by the visit of a famous bishop, the renowned Remigius of Reims. The town buzzed with excitement. The son of the count of Laon, Remigius was one of the most notable leaders of the Church in Gaul. His wisdom and erudition were known throughout Gaul, such that hosting him was considered a great honor.

The bishop arrived one fine spring day, an aristocratic-looking man mounted upon a splendid charger caparisoned in blue. The Christians cheered his arrival, while the Franks gawked in curiosity. "He certainly looks splendid!" said Floriana, watching the bishop's procession from the abbey gates.

"Indeed," said Genevieve, "but his true virtue is in his wisdom. They say he was made a bishop when he was only twenty-one, by demand of the people of Reims."

After paying homage to Duke Folmar and spending several days in counsel with Urscinius and the clergy, Remigius came to call on Genevieve at the abbey. Remigius had finely chiseled features and a hawkish expression, no doubt features inherited through his ancient bloodline that stretched back to the days of Rome's might. "Sister, your fame is spoken of even in the Church of Reims. Tales of your wonders are told far abroad."

"I have only done what I was bound to do," Genevieve said dismissively.

"There is great merit in that before Our Lord," said Remigius. "You have a certain way about you. You move mountains. Things that seem impossible become possible when the hand of Genevieve touches them."

"Did the eminent Bishop of Reims come all this way just to flatter me?" Genevieve said testily.

Remigius smiled. "Let me speak plainly, then. Clovis, by the grace of God, King of the Franks, wishes to take a wife."

"A noble thing," said Genevieve. "Has he chosen a bride?"

"Indeed he has, and his choice may interest you. He has entered an alliance with the King of Burgundy, who has given up his daughter, Clotilde, to be the wife of Clovis."

"The King of Burgundy? Why, the Burgundians are Christians! Clovis is to take a Christian wife?"

"Yes," Remigius nodded happily. "It seems we are to have a Catholic queen."

Genevieve clasped at her chest. "Imagine the influence she could have on the king! Perhaps the condition of Christians throughout the Frankish domains will improve."

"That is my hope," said Remigius. "The Church of Soissons has recently been plundered by the Franks. When I see the king, I must try to negotiate the return of the sacred vessels—chalices, patens, and a particularly splendid reliquary vase I hope I can retrieve intact. The Franks are not evil people so far as pagans go, but my constant protests against the pillaging of churches wear on me. I pray that Clotilde will soften the heart of Clovis, who in turn will soften the hearts of his people toward our faith."

"Here in Paris, we live in peace with them. Those sorts of incidents stopped long ago. We have even had a few Frankish converts."

"That is due to you, Genevieve," said the noble bishop. "You put people at ease. They trust you. It is a gift of Our Lord. And that is why I have come to see you."

"Oh?"

"The Lady Clotilde has been sent up from Burgundy and is preparing herself for matrimony at the tomb of Saint Denis the Martyr in Catulliacum. I am to go to Catulliacum to escort her to Paris at the behest of the king, where they are to be wed. It was my hope that you would accompany me to Catulliacum."

"Me? What value could I bring to such an endeavor? I do not involve myself in royal affairs."

Remigius laughed. "Don't involve yourself in royal affairs? What do you call that letter you sent to King Childeric?"

"That was . . . different."

"Whether you like it or not, you are renowned all over Gaul. Escorting the king's bride into Paris would be a tremendous honor for both Clotilde and Clovis. It would go a long way toward securing the good will of Clovis toward the Church."

"Perhaps," muttered Genevieve. "But I feel I am getting too old for these kinds of journeys."

"There and back in three days at most," the bishop insisted.

"I have duties here," Genevieve protested.

"There is another thing," said Remigius, lowering his voice. "Clotilde is . . . well . . . she's quite young. Only a teenager. She has been sent from the Christian court of Burgundy up into the wilds of pagan Francia. Her husband-to-be is not the gentlest of men."

"Of that, I am keenly aware."

"If I am being honest, I am not sure how happy she is about the arrangement," the bishop continued. "She submitted out of respect for her father and a desire to seal the alliance between the Franks and Burgundians, but I can't imagine she is excited about being married off to a violent pagan."

"I see," Genevieve nodded. "The poor girl is scared."

"I believe so. If you were to accompany me—"

"—say no more. I understand. I will consult with Bishop Urscinius on the matter right away."

"I have already spoken to Urscinius. He has given it his full blessing. We leave in two days' time."

It was a balmy May morning when Genevieve departed Paris for Catulliacum in the company of Remigius. Their horses lumbered at a leisurely gait, carrying them along the road northeast out of Paris, into the broad vineyards that spread out across the rolling hillsides. The grapes were beginning to bloom, clusters of flowers erupting everywhere in the broad leaves. Here and there, the form of a peasant could be seen stooping amongst the vines, working diligently in the morning sun. The day was warm and humid, the sky streaked with brooding dark clouds. Genevieve saw a rainbow momentarily glittering in the firmament above. It reminded her of the day so long ago when her mother had accompanied her to Paris in the train of girls from Nanterre who were to take vows before Bishop Vivianus. She looked down at her hands; they were older, thinning, notably worn, but the bronze ring on her finger still blazed as brightly as the day Duke Victorinus put it on.

Chapter 12

She Is No Saint

Once, in ancient times, there was a holy man named Denis. With the zeal of the faith burning in his breast, he crossed the Alps and sojourned among the Gallic people during the days of the pagan emperors of old. He wandered about the land, preaching until he pressed into the northernmost reaches of Rome's imperium, coming to the Roman town of Lutetia. There he made many converts among the Parisii, the Gallic pagans who dwelt in the dark, misty forests along Seine. His preaching sparked a fierce dissention among the pagans, troubling the peace of the settlement so much that the Roman authorities were compelled to put a stop to it. Invoking the imperial decrees against Christian clergy, the Romans condemned Denis to death. The holy man was taken outside the city to a hill venerated by the pagans. There, kneeling with hands folded in prayer, the saint's head was severed from his shoulders by a cruel Roman blade. Even this was unable to silence the witness of the holy man, for to the amazement of all, he picked his head up off the ground, held it aloft, and walked about with it, continuing to preach to the stunned pagans for some time before finally collapsing in death.

This is the story the locals always told, at any rate.

In Genevieve's day, the tomb of Saint Denis at Catulliacum was the site of a popular shrine. An old Roman church nestled cozily into the sloping hillside, marking the spot where the saint was entombed. A bustling town fanned out around the shrine, spreading down into the fields beyond. The older buildings were of stone and marble, while the surrounding houses were newer, stately timber structures with freshly thatched roofs.

"I came here once, shortly after I came to Paris," said Genevieve wistfully as she and Remigius approached Catulliacum on horseback. "It has changed much since then. The town has expanded considerably."

"The shrine of Saint Denis has always been popular," said Remigius, "but devotion seems to have grown since the coming of the Franks. I suspect that as the pagans overran Gaul, the Christian people wanted to cling to this place all the more. With old Christian Gaul being swept away in a tide of Frankish heathenism, these sorts of connections to our past are more important than ever."

"The Lady Clotilde was wise to choose Catulliacum as the place of her preparation before being wedded to Clovis," said Genevieve. "The prayers of Saint Denis will go with her."

"I do not know what the future holds," said Remigius pensively. "But I have met Lady Clotilde on several occasions. She is a young woman of excellent character with a refined sense of piety. God will surely not fail to use a woman as saintly as Clotilde for His glory."

"Saintly?" Genevieve said, raising her eyebrows.

Remigius smiled, shrugging a little.

Upon entering Catulliacum, they were told Clotilde was at the shrine. Remigius and Genevieve found her entourage standing about outside the chapel, a company of female attendants and a few Burgundian clergymen brought from home. "The princess is within the chapel, absorbed in prayer," said one of the Burgundian clerics with a dramatic flourish.

"Perhaps we should not impose upon her just yet?" said Remigius.

"If she wishes to be saintly and a Queen of the Franks, she must get used to being imposed upon," Genevieve said testily, dismounting her steed.

"Very well," sighed Remigius, "you go and speak with her. I will await you."

The shrine of Saint Denis was very old, its bulky limestone blocks greened with years of moss. Vines wound up the worn, old columns that flanked the front portal. Genevieve entered through the heavy oaken doors that segregated the holy place from the clamor of the outside world. The shrine's interior was swathed in shadow, light filtering in through a few narrow arched openings above the porticoes lining each side of the nave. Normally, the shrine would have been crowded with pilgrims, but today it was quite empty, cleared out so Princess Clotilde could pray in solitude.

Genevieve fell to her knees upon the cool flagstone and made the sign of the cross. The tomb itself rested at the east side of the chapel, marked by an old marble altar with the inscription *HIC CORPUS SANCTI DIONYSII MARTYRII REQUIESCIT*—"Here rests the body of holy Denis the Martyr." It was before that altar that Genevieve caught first sight of Clotilde.

The Burgundian princess seemed oblivious to Genevieve's entrance. Kneeling upon a cushion, her head veiled, vested in a colorful gown, the young woman gazed at the altar with a look of rapt abandon. Genevieve rose and approached the princess till she was looming over her. Still, Clotilde did not acknowledge her. Genevieve was struck with the awkwardness of the situation, struggling to find words. She knelt beside the young woman, crossed herself, and began her own prayers. For some time, the two women continued this way, side by side, mouths moving silently as each stared at the ancient tomb.

The altar was crowded with candles, upon it and around it, left by votaries seeking Denis's prayers. They bathed the sanctuary in a soft glow.

Candlelight always reminds me of grace, Genevieve thought. *Gentle and peaceful but persistent . . . enlightening.*

In front of the altar, a small opening in the floor was sealed off by a grille. The opening sunk down into darkness, leading eventually to the body of Denis himself. This was the *fenestella*, an opening through which the faithful could let down trinkets on a string and touch them to the sacred bones. Genevieve thought of the past, of all the thousands of pilgrims since antiquity who had knelt at this spot, dropping crosses and pendants into the blackness to establish a connection with the martyr. Then she thought of the future, of the coming of Christ at the end of days—when the trumpets would sound, when the call of the archangel would go forth and the dead would rise in glory. She envisioned the light of heaven blazing out of the dark hole, perhaps even the body of Denis himself emerging from it, glorified and radiant in the splendor of life undying.

Gradually, she lost herself in her prayers, her eyes closed, losing sense of time, forgetting everything but—

"—you must be Genevieve of Paris?"

Genevieve blinked and looked. Clotilde stared at her, a bright, brown-eyed girl with a round face and full lips. Genevieve collected herself. "Yes, I am Genevieve, Your Highness," she bowed from her knees.

Clotilde looked her up and down. "You are very plain," she said coolly. "I would not have taken you to be the legend people make of you."

"Well, the glory of the Christian is interior," Genevieve grinned wincingly. "And I am not quite the legend they say. I am just a woman who loves our sweet Christ."

Clotilde smiled but coldly. Though donned in royal regalia with elaborately braided hair beneath a transparent ornate veil, a patch of acne across her chin betrayed her youth as a teenage girl.

"Tell me, do you know Clovis? Have you met him?" Her voice was dispassionate and aloof.

"I do indeed," Genevieve said.

"Can you tell me of him?"

Genevieve's mind raced back to the awful day Paris fell, to Clovis's expressionless face as he hurled an ax through the skull of another human being for amusement.

"He is quite intense," Genevieve responded. "Of a very serious demeanor. A tall man with a full blond mustache."

"Typical Frank," Clotilde murmured.

"I've had the chance to speak with him on several occasions since he became king," Genevieve continued. "He is straightforward, very direct of speech. But he is not dull; he is quite clever, in fact."

"But is he *good*?" Clotilde entreated. Her voice wavered. There was a look of pleading in her eyes.

Genevieve smiled sadly. "He is the King of the Franks. He is what they need him to be."

Clotilde's head dropped. "I, too, will be what I need to be, then." She almost choked on the words.

"Clotilde, I know you are scared . . ." Genevieve reached her arm out and touched the princess's shoulder. Clotilde began to shake.

"What if he is awful?" she exclaimed. "What if he is a brutal savage? I'll be surrounded by pagans. How will I . . ." Her lips began to quiver, tears welled up in the corners of her eyes.

Genevieve felt a touch of compassion but also sadness at the young woman's plight. Still more, she felt a flash of anger.

You think you've got troubles, Princess? I'll bet you've never buried your parents or almost been murdered or watched someone you loved being carried off like a trophy.

"I cannot lie to you," Genevieve said curtly. "I will not imagine virtues for Clovis that he does not have. He is a Frank. What more do you want from me?"

Clotilde lost her composure, breaking into tears. "Can you say nothing to comfort me?"

Genevieve was stung by regret—the sense of having been handed something delicate and then breaking it through carelessness. "Forgive me!" she implored. "I have been harsh with my words. The king is rough, I will not deny. But I will say, since the first time I met Clovis, when he was but a lad, I thought there was something special about him. He can come across as severe and unfeeling, but I firmly believe there is more to him than that. I think if he had just a bit of light in his life, perhaps it would shine through more."

"Well, that's something," Clotilde said, composing herself.

Genevieve shifted uncomfortably; she had been kneeling on the flagstone for some time and was beginning to ache.

"What did you come here for?" she asked the girl, motioning to the altar. Clotilde turned her gaze to the candlelit marble slab, the crudely painted image of Saint Denis holding his own head upon the crumbling wall plaster, the rough-hewn cross that overlooked the altar and the kneeling women.

"I suppose I came here to find peace," Clotilde responded. "To seek God's consolation. To come to terms with this cross."

Genevieve knelt in silence for a time, then speaking with great delicacy, said, "I think, Princess, that it is best not to try to think of this as a cross you need to come to terms with."

"Why do you say this?" asked Clotilde. "This is an occasion of great anxiety for me. Does that not make it a cross?"

"The things that befall us in life, we cannot truly understand why they happen. Who can know the mind of God? They simply *are*. They fall on us like rain. We can no more pick our blessings and crosses than we could walk through a storm and avoid the raindrops. Sometimes, we cannot even discern the difference between a blessing and a cross. Things come into our lives that we take for crosses, and yet they can turn out to be blessings, and situations we imagine as blessings end up being crosses. Who can see all ends but God alone? The wheat and the tares grow together in this world until the great harvest at the end of time. It is very difficult to try to sort them out prematurely."

Clotilde nodded. "I see why people esteem your counsel so highly."

Genevieve blushed, though it was imperceptible in the flickering shadows. "Well, I have reflected much on this, for the better part of my life, really. I have spent days without number trying to make sense of my sufferings, which have been many. The only way I could get through them all was to just keep walking. Keep my eyes on that luminous horizon. And it made me see that where I am going is more important than where I have been."

"And where am *I* going? Where is God taking me?"

"It doesn't matter," Genevieve smiled.

"Doesn't matter? How can you say that?"

"What is salvation?" asked Genevieve.

"Eternal life with the Trinity," Clotilde replied.

"And when does eternal life begin?"

The princess considered this. "When we go to heaven?"

"No, it begins right *here*, right *now*. 'The kingdom of heaven is within you,' Our Lord says. If that is true, then every step you take on your journey—even the steps you will take when you leave this chapel—are part of that long road to glory. It does not matter what you encounter on that road; we all have our obstacles, and you will certainly have yours, as I have had mine. But your path is not mine, and mine is not yours. It's fruitless to compare the path you are on with how you imagine it should be."

"So, you are telling me to . . . let go of my preferences?"

"Stop fretting because life hasn't turned out the way you wanted. *Just let life happen*. Let it fall upon you like the rain. Let God give you what He will."

Clotilde smiled. Genevieve noticed there was now a brightness in her countenance, dim but discernible. Something within her had changed. She nodded gracefully. "I thank you for your wisdom, Genevieve of Paris. You've consoled me mightily. I beg, grant me a few more moments alone here before the Lord. I will meet you outside, and then we can depart for Paris."

"As you wish," Genevieve bowed. She made the sign of the cross and stood up. A little groan escaped her lips as she struggled to her feet. She bent her knee before the majesty of God, then departed in silence, leaving the princess to her prayers.

Outside the chapel, Remigius stood with the other attendants talking. When Genevieve came forth, he came to her swiftly. "How is she? What happened? You were in there for quite some time. Is all well?"

"All is well," said Genevieve, massaging her sore kneecaps. "She is no saint—but she will be one day."

"Praise God," Remigius responded, signing himself.

"Remigius, I have a favor to ask of you that I beg you not deny me."

"Anything."

"Please assign me a penance," Genevieve said.

"Oh? For what?"

"It matters not. Assign me a penance without knowing my fault."

"I cannot imagine you have committed any great fault," Remigius said.

"Don't imagine at all. Please, just give me a penance," Genevieve insisted.

"Very well," Remigius sighed. "Thirty days on bread and water."

A smile spread across Genevieve's face. Her eyes burned bright with gratitude. "Glory be to Christ," she said, clasping her hands in joy.

Chapter 13

The Lord Is a Man of War

Clovis and Clotilde were wed on the steps outside the grand portal of Saint Etienne. Clotilde's father had insisted on a Christian wedding for his daughter as part of the arrangement, and thus, Clovis yielded to the strange rite he cared little for and understood even less. Genevieve and her sisters stood in the mass of people around the church to watch the nuptials. She kept her hands folded in her sleeves, mouthing prayers silently while the bride and groom exchanged vows. *He's so big*, Genevieve marveled at Clovis. No longer the petulant youth from years ago, he was now tall and robust with thick arms and an impressive mustache. Like his predecessors, he wore his hair long. It tumbled over his shoulders and down his back, a sign of the magical powers the Franks believed were vested in the bloodline of their leaders.

Bishop Urscinius pronounced their union and made the sign of the cross over the couple. The Frankish entourage gathered at the ceremony roared their approval, clashing their axes upon their shields.

"Leave it to the Franks to show up to a wedding armed," Sister Floriana muttered.

Genevieve smiled but said, "There is a certain charm to it. I used to find the Frankish attachment to their weapons distasteful, but now I see that, to them, a weapon is not just for killing."

"Oh?" said Floriana. "What else do you use a weapon for?"

"For the Franks, it is everything. It is a sign of a man's valor. It is a way to show approval. It is a tool. It is a sign of rank. It is often an inheritance from his father. It embodies everything the Franks hold to be important. It is a great honor for the king and queen to hear this racket at their nuptials."

"You have certainly changed since the days when you viewed them as filthy barbarians!" Floriana marveled.

Genevieve shrugged. "How can we not change? Life is constantly moving."

The days after the royal wedding were indeed a time of great change in Paris. Bishop Urscinius fell ill suddenly and died. It was as if joining Clovis and Clotilde was the final jewel in the crown of his episcopacy before divesting himself of his mortal labors. The clergy of the cathedral elected a man named Apedinus, an old Parisian priest who had spent many years preaching among the Franks—and had the scars to show for it.

But by far the most sweeping change was Clovis's decision to move his capital from Tournai to Paris. This announcement brought a flurry of activity to the city such as Genevieve had never seen. The old civic basilica where the Roman dukes had once ruled was revamped to serve as Clovis's court. Teams of workmen toiled nonstop, repairing the crumbling structure and clearing debris from the overgrown forum that fronted the building. The wooden rampart that surrounded the city was also reinforced where needed.

Besides the physical changes, Genevieve also noticed there were simply more Franks in the city. News that Clovis intended to make his court there drew an influx of Frankish notables who wanted to be close to the seat of Frankish power. Of course, these days it was getting harder and harder to tell the Franks and Gallo-Romans apart; the old Gallo-Romans had long ago started wearing the trousers and colorful tunics of the Franks, while the Franks had begun adopting some of the more cultured mannerisms of their Christian subjects.

After the arrival of Clovis's family, Genevieve often called upon Queen Clotilde, more out of obligation than affection. They spent many afternoons together in the queen's chambers, sometimes in the company of Remigius or Bishop Apedinus as they discussed ecclesiastical affairs. King Clovis, too, paid them frequent visits, asking questions about the Christian faith. Genevieve found these conversations well-meaning but clumsy. The Franks simply valued different things than the Christians; Clovis in particular had a difficult time grasping the Christian virtue of humility. When Remigius spoke to him of the crucifixion of Jesus, Clovis pounded his fist on the table. "If I were there with my Franks, I would have stopped it! I would not have let him be crucified!" Genevieve smirked upon seeing Remigius's expression as he tried to respond to this noble but misguided declaration.

Usually, however, it was Genevieve and Clotilde alone. The two would make pleasantries until Clotilde inevitably began to unload her frustrations about life. Genevieve would sit nearby, weaving on a loom while she let the young woman pour out her soul. She mostly listened in these moments, speaking only to interject a word of advice or encouragement here and there. Genevieve struggled with Clotilde; she seemed mired in her own troubled thoughts, unable to break from her anxiety. Such had never been Genevieve's way. When Genevieve saw a mountain, she thought, "I want to see what's on the other side." When Clotilde saw a mountain, she thought, "It's so big, I will never be able to get over it!" At least that's the way Genevieve imagined the distinction. She had a difficult time empathizing with Clotilde's approach to things. She would often pray silently while Clotilde rambled on.

Lord, give this woman your comfort. Give her heart peace.

Despite their differing temperaments, the initial coolness between the two women thawed. Beneath Clotilde's troubled exterior, Genevieve perceived a young woman of true faith who wanted only to do good. Though she vacillated between displays of flamboyant piety and agonized despondency, gold shined between these extremes. She simply needed more balance. Once Genevieve understood this, affection warmed in her heart, and with time, she came to love Clotilde in a motherly way. This love would prove to be a grace, for tragedy quickly marred the domestic life of Clovis and Clotilde

Clotilde and Clovis were blessed with their first child not long after they were wed. Influenced by the good examples of Clotilde, Remigius, and Genevieve, Clovis gave his permission to allow the child to be baptized a Christian. The boy, Ingomer, was accordingly baptized, but immediately after the ritual, the child fell ill and died. Clovis was furious.

"You convinced me to put my firstborn son into your magic water, and it killed him!" he shouted at his wife, storming through her chambers. "What kind of twisted religion is this you push upon me? Never again will a child of mine go near your cursed water!"

Clotilde summoned Genevieve, and upon her arrival, broke down into the elder woman's arms, sobbing uncontrollably. Her heart was broken from the death of her child, from the wrath of her husband, and from the insults hurled at her religion. "He stormed out and said he could not look at my face," Clotilde wept. "What will become of me now? How will I live like this?"

Genevieve pressed the young woman's head to her bosom. "We have done all we can," she said gently. "If God wants the heart of the king changed, He will have to speak to Clovis in a way that *he* understands. Leave the future to Him. For now, let us just commend ourselves to His care."

The queen nodded, sniffling, and the two women knelt together, facing the crucifix that adorned the east wall of

Clotilde's chambers. "*Pater noster, qui es in cœlis, sanctificétur nomen tuum,*" began Genevieve, uttering a prayer familiar to every Christian soul, but here invested with new layers of meaning in light of the queen's circumstance. Clotilde closed her eyes, hands folded before her, mouthing the words of the prayer silently while tears pooled in the corners of her eyes and trickled down her cheeks.

Things were cold between Clovis and Clotilde for some time after Ingomer's death. Clovis distracted himself with matters of war as another pagan tribe, the Alemanni, were pushing into Frankish lands from the east. Their looting grew so severe that Clovis summoned his army to go east and confront them. Frankish warriors converged on Paris throughout June, heeding Clovis's call to arms. The surrounding plains were again cluttered with Frankish tents and the watchfires of warriors preparing for war. The last time Genevieve had witnessed such a sight, it was a specter of terror; now these same rough, mustachioed warriors were allies and defenders of Paris.

Genevieve and her sisters lined up with the clergy of the city outside the gates to watch Clovis depart with his army the first week of June. It was a cacophony of diverse sounds, the clergy intoning the second Psalm in the deep and sonorous chants of the Church, while the Frankish rabble roared, beating spears, axes, pots, and pans in the belief that the noise would attract the attention of their gods and convince them to look favorably upon their king. The soldiers—most of them mounted—processed out the gates in a long line, joining with the forces already mustered on the plain. Clovis rode in the middle of the column, his long hair wound in several elaborate braids falling down his back. His face was grim and his posture statue-like, conveying a sense of immovability. The king glanced at Genevieve and her sisters as he passed. She lifted her hand in greeting, the morning sun glinting off her ring. For a moment, his stern countenance broke, his hairy lip turning up with a slight smile.

The next days rolled by lazily. The land settled into a hot summer; farmers sweated in the fields while Parisians swatted away the hordes of flies that pestered the streets. Genevieve and her sisters toiled in the abbey gardens by day and spent their evenings in prayer, gathered before the Lord in the cathedral—and afterward continuing in cells, meditating silently in the gloom of the night. All the while the queen brooded behind the walls of her keep, praying and waiting for word of her husband.

By the end of June, rumors began to swirl about the countryside. The news was confusing at first; some said the king had suffered a disastrous defeat, others that he had secured an astonishing victory. Then came messengers from the Frankish forces, bringing more reliable information—the king had won a victory against the Alemanni but at great cost. Many men were wounded and killed. It was unclear whether the king was alive or not.

The apparent severity of the losses and uncertainty about Clovis dampened the joy of the victory. Bishop Apedinus held a procession through the city, beseeching the Trinity for the life and health of the king. The Franks watched in muted curiosity as the Christians marched through the dirty streets in song, led by an army of white-robed clergy incensing the Parisian air.

On the first of July, messengers came to the cathedral, announcing the return of the army, but the king was not among them. It seemed that he and the bulk of the soldiers had chosen to go to Reims instead of returning to Paris. Genevieve, upon hearing the news, expected to be summoned by the queen, and it was not long before the summons came. Genevieve thought she would find Clotilde in disarray, but when she was admitted to the queen's chambers, she found her instead puzzling over a scrap of parchment.

"My lady, what is this you read?"

"As the Lord lives, I am not sure," said Clotilde. "Please read this, Genevieve, and tell me your thoughts."

Genevieve took the parchment and squinted—something she generally did now when she read. The note, scribbled in sloppy, hasty Latin, read, "The king requests your presence in Reims. He is well and praises God for his victory. Find him in the house of Remigius. *Christus vincit*."

"The king praises God for his victory? *Christus vincit*?" Genevieve said, puzzled.

"What does this mean?" Clotilde asked.

"It seems . . . it seems he acknowledges Jesus Christ."

"Could he have truly found faith?" Clotilde mused. "Or was this letter written by some overzealous monk? I do not even know from whom this came. The messenger said only that the king had ordered it be sent."

"Will you go to Reims?" inquired Genevieve.

"Of course I shall!" Clotilde declared. "I must get to the bottom of this. And I'd like your company. That is, if you're willing."

"I am willing, my lady," Genevieve nodded. "The king's good is our good as well. And it's been a while since I have had an adventure."

While Genevieve entrusted the care of the abbey to Sister Floriana, a traveling party was hastily assembled, consisting of Clotilde, several attendants, and a dozen Frankish cavalrymen. Genevieve joined them at the city gates, and the party set out at once. Even at a brisk pace, the journey would be three days. The horses kept a hurried gait across the expansive farm country that stretched between Paris and Reims. Even had there been leisure for chat, Clotilde was troubled and in no mood to talk. Genevieve bounced silently in the saddle, praying to the rhythm of the horse's trot. At night, they made camp under tents of hide and upon piles of fur clustered about a hastily erected watchfire. Genevieve dozed off to sleep under the watch of a gaggle of Frankish soldiers sitting around the fire, drinking.

How strange, she thought as she observed their rugged, mustachioed faces, taking turns telling stories as they laughed in the fire's glow. *I never imagined I would fall asleep under the protection of Frankish soldiers or find comfort in their presence. How odd life is . . .*

Genevieve was awake before dawn, chilled and clammy from the morning dew. She arose stiff and aching, her joints burning. Stepping out into the dampened grass, she forced her rigid body to its knees and began her morning prayers. She winced as a searing pain shot up her back. She recalled the old days of her youth when she used to bound about the countryside around Nanterre and in the slopes of Mont Valérien, barefoot in perfect wholeness. Now her body begrudged even her attempt to simply rest outdoors, punishing it with wracking pain.

They were soon on the move again and came upon Reims on the evening of the third day. Genevieve and Clotilde heard King Clovis was secluded with Remigius in the episcopal residence. The two women were ushered into the bishop's chambers, where Remigius and Clovis sat before a great fireplace, talking.

When the women were announced, Clovis rose swiftly and rushed to his wife. His eyes were wild and bright with a look neither Clotilde nor Genevieve had ever seen. He grasped Clotilde's hands and held them to his breast. "Your God has granted me victory!"

"What is this you speak of?" Clotilde asked.

"I found the Alemanni near a place called Tolbiac, as you go up toward the Rhine," he began. "I caught them with their backs to the river and ordered the attack. I thought they were mine. But the Alemanni were stronger than I thought. They pressed us hard, and a great many of my Franks fell."

"We heard there had been a terrible slaughter," said Genevieve. "We have been praying nonstop for your well-being and that of the army."

Clovis looked at Genevieve and grasped her shoulder firmly in his powerful hand. "You don't know how much your prayers have accomplished! In the heat of battle, I found myself cut off, surrounded by the Alemanni. So, I called out to the gods of the Franks"—here Clovis clasped his hands and gazed upward theatrically, acting out his supplication—"but the gods of the Franks did not help me!"

"What happened next?" Clotilde said, trembling.

"Feeling an emptiness as I called upon my gods, I turned instead to the Christian God. I said, 'Jesus Christ, who my wife says is the Son of God, I beg for your help. If you give me victory over my enemies, I will believe in you and be baptized. I want to believe, but first I must be saved.'"

Genevieve's hand flew to her mouth. Clotilde gasped. The image of King Clovis ever uttering such words was inconceivable to both women.

"And then"—by now, the king was quite animated, acting out the battle before them—"just as I prayed, the King of the Alemanni was killed! I saw the whole thing. Ragrim, one of my chiefs, he buried an ax right in his head! It was glorious, Clotilde! You should have seen the look on his face when he took the strike. His skull was *shattered*. And the blood—"

"—yes, Husband, we understand, the man was killed," Clotilde interjected impatiently. "But what happened next?"

"Yes, forgive me. When the Alemanni saw their king fall, they panicked and tried to flee. But of course, I had them with their backs to the Rhine, so they had nowhere to go. When they saw they were trapped, they threw down their weapons and surrendered. They asked for mercy and peace. I normally would not grant such favor, but I was so awestruck at the effectiveness of my own prayer that I granted them clemency. And thus, we had victory."

Genevieve made the sign of the cross. Clotilde, shaking, said, "Husband, have you come to faith in Jesus Christ?"

"Yes, dear wife!" He seized her by the waist and drew her to him. His face was flushed, his eyes full of exuberance. "I had to tell you! I had a scribe pen that letter and sent it to you so we could be reunited here."

Clotilde beamed, but her lips quivered and soon she was crying, though now in happiness. Clovis pulled her to him, stroking her long blond braids. "I know I have been harsh to you," he said softly. "For that, I am sorry. And that I did not return to Paris. But I needed to see Remigius right away to tell him what occurred and to seek his counsel."

Remigius, who had been standing by silently beaming, spoke up. "The king seeks baptism. He is going to confer with his lords, and so long as there is no serious opposition, we will prepare for the ceremony at once."

Hearing this, Clotilde's tears turned to laughter. Genevieve dropped to her knees, the pain of kneeling on stone overwhelmed by the sense of sheer exultation. In a spontaneous burst of jubilation, she cried out the words of Moses after the Israelites had crossed the Red Sea: "I will sing to the Lord, for He has triumphed gloriously; the horse and His rider He has thrown into the sea. The Lord is a man of war; the Lord is His name."

Chapter 14

The Alpha and the Omega

The squares of Reims were decorated with tapestried canopies to accommodate the overflow of visitors thronging the city for the king's baptism. Bouquets of flowers fixed in wreaths of myrtle beautified the doors of houses. Within the cathedral of Reims, Genevieve worked tirelessly with the Christian women of the city to prepare the church for the rite. The nave was adorned with white curtains that blew in the summer breeze. The baptistery, an octagonal alcove jutting out from the apse, was filled with lilies clustered around the ancient stone font where the water of life would bestow new birth upon the King of the Franks.

On the great day, the cathedral was packed with spectators, some Christian, some pagan, all there alike to witness the spectacle of Clovis professing the faith of Christ. Genevieve knelt beside Clotilde in the choir adjacent to the baptistery. Clouds of thick incense hung in the air as the king processed through the nave, barefoot and dressed in the simple garb of a penitent. Behind him followed scores of his most

loyal warriors, those pledged to follow him in life or death who agreed to accompany their king right into the waters of baptism. Remigius awaited the king in the baptistery in full episcopal regalia, surrounded by candles of fragrant odor burning brightly. The king entered the baptistery with head downcast, hair unbraided, flowing down his back.

"Bow your head, O King," began Remigius. "Adore what thou hast spurned, and spurn what thou hast adored." Clovis bent his head over the baptismal font while the bishop dipped a seashell into the water and poured it thrice upon the crown of his head, pronouncing the ancient formula of baptism, "Clovis, *ego te baptízo in nómine Patris, et Fílii, et Spíritus Sancti.*" His long hair had to be held behind his head by attendants, lest it dip into the sacred font.

All that day, Remigius administered the sacrament to Clovis's warriors. As the sun began to dip behind the western hills and the cathedral sunk into soft shadow, the newly baptized were vested in robes of white. Bearing lighted candles, they processed out of the church, flanked by clergy chanting sonorously. The smells of the honeyed candles and incense and sacred chrism enchanted both the new and the old Christians.

Clotilde and Genevieve both wept at the spectacle. "It's as if we sit in the very odor of paradise," said Clotilde, wiping her eyes. Genevieve put her arm around the young queen.

The festivities continued all that week, with plenty of feasting and celebrating. Christian subjects of Clovis streamed into the city to present him with gifts for the special occasion. The king was humbled by these professions of homage from subjects whom he had hitherto considered suspect because they were not Franks. Meanwhile, Franks throughout Reims came to the churches, seeking instruction and baptism. "There is neither Jew nor Greek, slave nor free," mused Genevieve when she saw these good things. "You are all one in Christ Jesus." Indeed, the Gospel of Christ was slowly obliterating the old distinction between Frank and Roman.

The years following Clovis's conversion were years of gentle intoxication for Genevieve. It seemed that at long last, after a lifetime of hardship, things finally began to fall into place. Paris was thriving, and though the Franks did not give up their warlike customs, at least the wars were further away, on the frontiers of the Frankish dominion. Regularity returned to life. Genevieve spent her days in prayer or working with her sisters in the convent gardens. A steady stream of visitors continued to call upon Genevieve, and she received them gracefully, year by year aging into the venerable matron of Christian Paris.

The convent in Paris was swollen with postulants, many of them Frankish women. Sister Floriana, now herself an aged matron of spiritual insight, told Genevieve, "The Frankish converts who seek our abbey show a zeal for the faith I have seldom seen."

Indeed, the sisters took in so many that Genevieve was compelled to approach King Clovis and Duke Folmar for new land upon which to expand the abbey. She called upon the king and was admitted to the royal stables adjacent to the king's keep where Clovis stood grooming his horses. "Grace to the king," Genevieve said, bowing. "I have come to speak with you about the matter of the abbey expansion."

The king turned briefly before going back to his horse. "I have other work for you, Genevieve," he told her curtly while brushing the mane of his steed. "I want you to leave this business of the abbey to others."

"The abbey is my primary concern," Genevieve responded.

"Not anymore," said Clovis. Genevieve shuffled uncomfortably; though the king had changed much since his youth, sometimes he still displayed the brusqueness that had so annoyed her when she first met him as a boy during the siege of Paris.

"Paris has grown much in past few years," Clovis continued. "The settlements have spilled outside the old walls to the other side of the Seine."

"It is so," said Genevieve. "The king's presence here gives this city great importance."

"My wife, Clotilde, says a growing city needs a new church. I intend to construct a grand church in the newer section of the city. It will be dedicated to Saint Peter and Saint Paul. What do you think of this?"

"My lord, it pleases me greatly that you seek to honor God in this way. But why do you ask my advice? Should you not go to the bishop?"

"For consent, I go to the bishop. For vision, I go to you."

"What do you mean by this?"

"I want you to oversee the construction of the church," Clovis said.

Genevieve took a pleading step forward. "Oh, my king, I am not fit for such a task," she protested. "I am an old woman now. It is enough that I have to see to the expansion of the abbey and the management of my sisters."

"I told you, we'll leave the abbey expansion to someone else. I must have you working on this new endeavor."

"But I am no architect, nor engineer!"

"The architects and engineers will handle the details," the king said, now visibly annoyed. "But I want you to give us the vision—to select the site, draw out its footings, direct the architects on how it should look."

Genevieve sighed. "It is not that I don't appreciate the king's offer—"

"—then accept it," Clovis snapped.

Genevieve's legs lost their strength. She sat upon a nearby stool. "When I was young, I used to walk the countryside around Paris, calling on all the farmsteads," she said wistfully. "Back when you Franks had not yet taken over everything. Those were interesting times. I often felt like responsibility for the survival of the Church in Paris was entirely upon my shoulders."

"You were bold," Clovis said admiringly. "I remember the day you came to my father on the road outside Paris during the siege."

"It was a misty morning," Genevieve mused.

"You and your women came to plead for your city. You were imaginative and brave. That's the Genevieve I want right now."

"Your Majesty, building a church takes time. I may not live long enough to see it completed."

"Then you'd better not waste any time," the king said.

Genevieve bowed her head. "I see the king is inflexible, as always. The heart of the king is in the hand of the Lord. I will do as you request."

The king smiled victoriously. "It will be magnificent."

Genevieve returned to the abbey and spent hours praying alone before the altar. She gazed at the crucifix. *"Give me strength, O Lord,"* she whispered. *"Help me see this task through to completion. Let thy name not be shamed on my account. Give me your vision."*

The work was agonizing. Imparting her ideas to a crew of engineers and architects proved exacting and took her away from the abbey more than she liked. Furthermore, despite the king's assurance, Genevieve found herself enmeshed in a thousand details she had neither expertise nor interest in: negotiating disputes between the stonemasons and the architects, making sure materials promised by the court were delivered on time, haggling over prices with carpenters, seeking out quarries for better quality stone. She became, in effect, the foreman of the project which dragged on for several years.

"The king is killing me slowly," Genevieve said to Floriana one Sunday as the two walked along the Seine. "I'd rather have taken my chances with Attila the Hun on the battlefield of Châlons than spend another day quibbling over stonemasons' wages. These Franks are good at fighting but have a thing or two to learn about working together on a construction project. I don't even understand why the king wanted me to undertake this. He knows I'm not long for this world."

Floriana chuckled. "You really don't see, do you? Are you that humble?"

"What do you mean?" Genevieve asked incredulously.

"You are not long for this world. Where do you think you will be buried when you pass?"

Genevieve's eyes widened. "What?"

"Yes," Floriana said, "the king is compelling you to build your own tomb. Then when you are gone, Paris will have a shrine to the great Saint Genevieve! A place she herself built and within which her mortal remains are vested. Think of the pilgrimages that will come here! Think of the wealth that will flow into Paris!"

"Hush!" Genevieve blurted out. "Do you think it makes me happy to hear such things?"

"I'm sorry, Mother," Floriana said, casting her eyes down. "I did not mean to make light—"

"—I forgive you," said Genevieve, making the sign of the cross over the penitent sister. "Anyway, I believe I will go over to the construction site and see how things are progressing," she said, changing the subject.

"Shall I accompany you?"

"Bless you, Floriana, but no. I think I shall go alone today. I want to spend some time in contemplation."

Genevieve made her way over the bridge that spanned the Seine and followed the dusty roads northeast out of town. The way seemed longer than it did in her youth. Seemed longer than it did even the prior year.

I'm slower than I used to be, she thought. *Soon I'll have to take a carriage just to get anywhere within the city in less than a day!*

The site she had chosen for the Church of Saint Peter and Saint Paul was located on a forested hillock that gently sloped up to the northeast of the newer neighborhoods. Genevieve liked this part of town; everything was wider, and the streets were not yet trodden down into a muddy morass. The houses, too, were more uniform, almost all in the Frankish style: squat timber buildings with towering triangular roofs covered in thatch. A fair number of these newer inhabitants of Paris were Christianized Franks, as evidenced by the rough wooden crosses occasionally seen affixed to the pinnacles of the roofs.

It was late afternoon when she came at last to the site of the new church. Being Sunday, the workers were all gone. The half-completed structure stood like a silent sentinel overlooking the town. The façade of solid brick was supported by two buttresses on either side of the arched portal. The wall turned into a vast triangular pediment as it went up toward the roofline, the façade broken only by a few smaller arched windows to admit light. The roof was not yet completed, and the octagonal baptistery on the rear was still in construction, but it was complete enough for Genevieve to take pride in it.

The old woman stepped through the portal and into the nave. The polished stone floor was illumined with beams of sunlight that streamed down through the rafters, open to the sun. She smiled and tilted her head upward, catching the warmth of the day upon her brow. The area had a quiet peacefulness, like she remembered of the beloved Green Circle of her youth. In that moment, as peace enveloped her heart, she forgot all the tedium and frustration which the project had brought her. Instead, she felt only gratitude that she, a poor, barefoot peasant girl from Nanterre, should have become such a vessel to do the work of God.

The sanctuary's altar would come later, but the elevated dais upon which it would sit was already fashioned. There, Genevieve saw an unexpected lump. She squinted.

Is that a person?

She stepped forward cautiously, avoiding the loose stones and tools left scattered about the floor. It was indeed a person, draped in black, laying upon the sanctuary dais.

"You there . . ." Genevieve called out, "this is no place for napping!"

She crept closer, now within a few paces. The figure was completely covered in black cloth, even the face. "Wake up!" she exclaimed. She ascended the steps to the dais and prodded the figure with her foot. It was stiff as if dead. "Oh, dear Lord," she said, crossing herself. She looked with pity on the dead stranger and noticed that the body was laid out in the exact location where the high altar would stand.

"An ideal place to die," she said to herself.

She bent down and pulled back the cloth. To her great horror, she saw her own face looking back at her, eyes closed in death, skin pale and blotchy. Genevieve shrieked as she fell back. She looked away, closing her eyes, shaking her head, trying to regain her wits. When she managed the courage to look back, the image had vanished.

The Church of Saint Peter and Saint Paul was finally consecrated with great solemnity in the third summer of construction. Relics from Rome were brought in, and the bishops of Paris, Reims, and the other great cities of the Frankish kingdom were all in attendance. Genevieve assisted at the first Mass celebrated in the new edifice. An ornately carved altar of stone decorated with an ornamental screen stood upon the spot where she had seen the vision of her own deceased body. She knelt in prayer while the Bishop of Paris elevated the Sacred Host, proclaiming the flesh of Christ upon the altar. Tears trickled down Genevieve's dry and wrinkled cheeks as she received the Body of Christ.

When the Mass ended, Genevieve stood in conversation with Queen Clotilde, now a buxom woman with five young children.

"You are to be commended on what you have accomplished here in this sacred place," the queen said.

"It is you who deserves thanks," said Genevieve humbly. "This church was your idea. And had it not been for your example—your very presence in this kingdom—we would not be where we are today."

Clotilde bowed her head slightly. "Hearing this from such a venerable woman does me great honor."

Genevieve smiled briefly, but a moment later her eyes glazed over, and she seemed distant, preoccupied with something far away, something visible only in her mind's eye, hidden from everyone else.

"Genevieve?" said Clotilde.

Genevieve remained transfixed. Then just as suddenly as it had left, the gleam returned to her eyes, and she gazed again at the queen.

"Are you all right?" Clotilde asked.

"My lady," Genevieve said slowly, "you may have great troubles in this life. Things may not unfold according to your plans. Those you love may disappoint you and turn aside to other paths. These things you must be prepared for."

"Of what do you speak?" Clotilde demanded.

"But we must know that grace is always there, always working. It moves as constant as time, as ever present as the air we breathe. The evils we encounter in life do not negate it; rather, they create the space for it to work."

"Why do you tell me this?" Clotilde said, beginning to shake.

Genevieve's eyes glistened with tears. "If you could only see the gentleness of God's providence! His plans are carried out through us—through the people we meet, the places we go, the decisions we make. Always remember that, my dearest Clotilde. The grace of God is always with us, and as long as we give ourselves to it, then it matters not what temporal misfortune befalls us, for we are always in His will."

"Genevieve, if you are trying to warn me of something, please say it plainly!"

Genevieve smiled again, her face bright as the sun and full of life. She lifted her hand and removed the old polished bronze ring from her finger. Taking the queen's hand, she slipped it upon Clotilde's finger. "This ring was given to me long ago, in another life. It once belonged to a virgin of Paris before it was given to me. All these long years, I have worn it. See the little crosses that run around the band? I have taken to running my fingers over this ring in difficult moments, this little band of crosses with no beginning and no end. Just like Our Lord, the Alpha and the Omega. I am going to a place where I will no longer need it. I wish for you to keep it as a token of my affection. When you look upon it, please say a prayer for me."

Clotilde struggled to understand the moment but admired the ring. Its polished sheen had long ago dulled, the bronze slowly turning green. But the crosses upon the band were clearly discernible. "I will pray for you," she said solemnly, "though I think it is all of us who will be seeking your prayers before long."

Genevieve touched the queen's cheek tenderly. "Elijah left a double portion of his spirit when Elisha took his cloak. I pray whatever grace God has given me, His poor servant, will be doubled in you now"—and she clasped Clotilde's hands and folded them within her own—"for your own soul and for the good of our people."

"For the good of our people," Clotilde repeated.

The two women stood there, the virgin and the queen, the old and the young, in a moment of blissful communion while the church bells rang out joyfully above them.

Chapter 15

A Word of Wisdom

A small party of mounted travelers wound its way down the dusty road from the hilly countryside. Their pace was leisurely, for this was not a journey of state but of pilgrimage. At the head of the caravan sat an old woman, shriveled and hunched upon her steed and draped in a thick cloak to guard her meager form against the bluster of September's winds.

A blond-headed man on foot led the old woman's horse, bridle in hand.

"Deodatus," the old woman croaked, "how much further?"

"If we keep up this pace, we should make the town of Blois by nightfall," the man said. "We'll reach Tours tomorrow afternoon."

The woman sighed.

"Mother Genevieve, do you find the rigors of the journey difficult?" a young woman asked.

"No, Sister Lanthegild, I find the journey just to my tastes," answered Genevieve. "In fact, it is invigorating to be on the open road again. I ask Deodatus not because I am impatient to reach our journey's end but rather because I hoped we might have some time before us yet."

"You always enjoyed a good adventure, Mother," Lanthegild smiled.

The old woman chuckled. "It's true. My life seems to have been one adventure after another."

"I've heard many stories of the deeds you did when you were younger."

"I used to be a shepherdess in Nanterre. Did I ever tell you the story, Floriana?"

"Oh, Mother, I am Lanthegild," said the sister tenderly.

"Oh . . . yes, forgive me," Genevieve said, recalling her dear friend's recent death. "You are Lanthegild?"

"That's right, Mother."

"And that man there, he is Deodatus, Dalmatia's son?"

"Yes, Mother."

"And we are going on pilgrimage to the shrine of Saint Martin in Tours?" asked Genevieve.

"Yes, Mother. You promised the queen that you would make a pilgrimage there to pray for the success of the council and the king's work with the Frankish Church."

"Yes, I remember now. Thank you, Lanthegild."

The little party continued along the road for some time. Genevieve mouthed prayers silently as the horse lurched slowly up the road. She found it hard to focus, though. Her mind wandered, and everything she saw or heard reminded her of some memory from a hazy past.

Looking to the west, she saw, beyond the gently sloping hills, the blue ribbon of the Loire River winding its way toward the sea. The sun was bright, the clear blue sky broken by only a few wisps of cloud floating like cotton strands in the upper reaches of the heavens. Now and then, a gust of wind would sweep across the countryside, billowing Genevieve's cloak and rippling across the field grasses in waves of silver.

The green fields were broken up by occasional walls of fieldstone, within which the local shepherds penned their sheep. Genevieve smiled at the sight of the animals dotting the landscape. "Did I ever tell you I used to be a shepherdess?"

"Yes, Mother," said Lanthegild patiently. "I have heard the story."

"Ah, of course." Genevieve returned to her interior world, thoughts, prayers, memories, and sentiment all folding in upon one another as her imagination roamed whither it willed, like an exuberant puppy let off its leash.

"Mother Genevieve, riders approach," said Deodatus. The man's voice roused Genevieve. Looking up, she saw a party of three horsemen trotting up the road, draped in fine cloaks, evidencing a high station.

"Are they Frankish lords?" asked Lanthegild.

"They are too well groomed to be Frankish lords," Genevieve said more to herself, squinting to get a better look at the men. "And no mustaches. I'd venture they are ecclesiastics."

The three riders halted before Genevieve's party. "Hail, Mother!" said one of them, raising his hand in greeting. "We see you are religious sisters. Praise be to Christ. I am Quintianus, Bishop of Rodez. My brother bishops and I are bound for Orléans to attend the council summoned by King Clovis."

"Peace to you, Quintianus," Genevieve said. "I am Genevieve of Paris, and these are sisters and servants of our abbey. We are bound for Tours, to worship at the shrine of Saint Martin."

"Blessed Genevieve!" Quintianus said, bowing. "Your fame precedes you. We have all heard of your great works. But forgive me, I was not aware you were living still."

Genevieve giggled girlishly. "Well, I am eighty-six years old this year, so though I am not dead yet, I am certainly closer to it than I've ever been."

"Mother," said Bishop Quintianus, "pardon my forwardness, but I must ask—since I was a young man, I have heard the tale of how you went before King Childeric and convinced him to provision grain to feed the city during the siege. I have always been enchanted by this story, and I wonder if you might give me your own account so I can hear it from your own lips?"

"Yes!" interjected one of the other bishops. "Or the healing miracles you worked on your journeys through the countryside!"

"Is it true that you once knew the great Saint Patrick of Ireland?" the third added.

A look of puzzlement came across Genevieve's face. "Yes, yes, but . . . it's hard to remember it all," she stammered. "Let me see . . ."

"My lords, Mother Genevieve is old and tired," Lanthegild interrupted. "We are trying to make Blois by sunset and would prefer to continue on."

"Ah, very well," said Quintianus regretfully. "I pray thee, then, Mother, give us a word of wisdom to feed our spirits, and we shall be on our way to Orléans.

"A word of wisdom, eh?" Genevieve withdrew into the recesses of her mind, searching the treasury of all the knowledge she'd ever gained, all the wise words anyone had ever spoken to her. A jumble of faces paraded across her memory: her parents, Deacon Mucianus, Germanus, Patricius, Vivianus, Urscinius, Floriana, and a great many others. But it was all a confusing muddle. She closed her eyes and shook her head to clear her thoughts. Then looking up, she beheld the green countryside, looking again at the sheep. Her mind became lucid, her eyes twinkled, and her face brightened. "I will tell you a word of wisdom," she finally said.

"Please, Mother," urged Quintianus.

"We are all but sheep gone astray, every one of us awaiting our shepherd," she said.

The three bishops bowed. "Well said, Mother," Quintianus replied. "May the shepherd of souls find us, each and every one. Pray for us, will you?"

Genevieve nodded and touched her heart. "And you for me."

With farewells made, the three bishops passed on north along the road to Orléans.

"Shall we continue, Deodatus?" asked Genevieve spryly.

"As you wish, Mother," the man said, taking her horse's reins and leading her forth. And all that afternoon, they ventured onward, following a dusty road, winding this way and that across the verdant countryside, meandering west toward an ever-receding horizon.

Afterword

Tradition says that Saint Genevieve died on January 3, although the year is disputed. Alban Butler, when composing his famous *Lives of the Saints*, estimated her death to be around the year 500; other historians say 511 or 512 is more likely.

After her death, Clovis did indeed have her interred in the Church of Saint Peter and Saint Paul, which had become an abbey and later a Benedictine monastery. Miracles were reported at the tomb, and the church became a popular pilgrimage site. Eventually, it was renamed in honor of Genevieve and was ever after known as the Abbey of Saint Genevieve.

It is uncertain what specific interactions Saint Genevieve and Queen Clotilde had, but it is almost certain that they knew one another. Shortly after Genevieve died, Clotilde commissioned a monk to write a *Vita*, a hagiographical biography of the saint's life, which is our primary source of information about her. This seems to indicate that Clotilde had a personal devotion to Genevieve, which perhaps unfolded not unlike what I have presented in this book. Of course,

Clotilde herself would go on to be venerated as a saint after her death as well.

By the Middle Ages, Saint Genevieve was honored as the patron saint of Paris. Along with Saint Denis and Saint Martin, she became one of the most beloved French saints. The abbey where her mortal remains were interred was remodeled and rebuilt many times, the last being under King Louis XV (d. 1774).

Genevieve's popularity aroused the ire of the French revolutionaries. Radicals seized her abbey in 1791 and renamed it the Pantheon, proposing to use it as a burial site for famous Frenchmen. Two years later, during the Reign of Terror, the saint's remains were exhumed and taken to the Place de Grève, where they were burnt in a spectacle of public repudiation of France's Catholic heritage. Despite this barbarous sacrilege, the faithful managed to save at least some of her relics. The abbey was returned to the Church in 1821 but went back and forth between ecclesiastical and government ownership during the various political upheavals that plagued France during the nineteenth century. It was not until 1885 that the abbey was definitively reconsecrated to Saint Genevieve. What remains of her relics have been returned to their traditional resting place within the crypt of the abbey.

Today Saint Genevieve is still venerated on her traditional feast day of January 3, the date of her death. Her popularity has not waned over the years; she is just as beloved now as she was in ancient times. The unique way in which her life combined a religious vocation with a very active apostolate provides an admirable model for the needs of today's Church. It is my hope that this book will help you learn to love Saint Genevieve as I have learned to love her—as well as grow in trust in the providence of God, who "causes all things to work together for good to those who love God, to those who are called according to *His* purpose" (Rom 8:28).